Growing Up

Growing Up
Life Behind the Chalkboard

Inspired by a True Story

Jessika C. Hearne

Copyright © 2017 by Jessika C. Hearne.

Library of Congress Control Number:		2017907900
ISBN:	Hardcover	978-1-5434-2441-6
	Softcover	978-1-5434-2440-9
	eBook	978-1-5434-2439-3

All rights reserved. No part of this book may be reproduced or transmitted in any form or by any means, electronic or mechanical, including photocopying, recording, or by any information storage and retrieval system, without permission in writing from the copyright owner.

This is a work of fiction. Names, characters, places and incidents either are the product of the author's imagination or are used fictitiously, and any resemblance to any actual persons, living or dead, events, or locales is entirely coincidental.

Any people depicted in stock imagery provided by Thinkstock are models, and such images are being used for illustrative purposes only.
Certain stock imagery © Thinkstock.

Print information available on the last page.

Rev. date: 05/23/2017

To order additional copies of this book, contact:
Xlibris
1-888-795-4274
www.Xlibris.com
Orders@Xlibris.com
760454

CONTENTS

Acknowledgements vii
Introduction xi

Chapter 1   Childhood Worries 1
Chapter 2   Hidden Secrets—Too Scared to Tell 5
Chapter 3   Breaking Point 9
Chapter 4   Silent Cries 15
Chapter 5   Escape 21
Chapter 6   Attempt to Fill a Void 25
Chapter 7   The Fight 31
Chapter 8   College Life and One Life Loss 37
Chapter 9   Sisterhood 43
Chapter 10   First Real Love 47
Chapter 11   Behind Most Smiles 51
Chapter 12   Is Enough Really Enough When You're Finally Fed Up? 59
Chapter 13   Happily Ever After and Many Happy Hours Needed ... 65
Chapter 14   First-Time Wife 75
Chapter 15   Resilience 81
Chapter 16   Lessons Learned: "Sweet Sixteen" 85
Chapter 17   So What! Now What? 89
Chapter 18   Chalkboard Talk from Musik Raine's Perspective 93
Chapter 19   God's Favor on Musik Raine 99
Chapter 20   Help More, Hurt Less 103

Index 107

ACKNOWLEDGEMENTS

TO GOD, THANK you for making life and everything possible.

To my spiritual leader, Bishop Leroy J. Woodard. Your Sunday-morning sermons are uplifting and inspirational. You are a realist. You speak on real life issues, and you are not afraid to put people in their place if they are wrong. You have prayed for me through so many situations throughout my life. Most importantly, you never judged me. Church people, in particular, will always be the first to judge. This is the quickest way to chase people away from the church. They are also quick to judge what people have on, who they are with, and/or who they may be messing with, just to have something to talk about. However, you are quick to put an end to all the madness. I have benefited greatly from your spiritual guidance.

You have a genuine heart to help people and have done an outstanding job with upholding and carrying on your father's legacy. Every year during Thanksgiving Day and Christmas Eve, you host the annual feeding where thousands of homeless families are given clothes, shoes, toys, and other basic necessities. Each year, you remind our church members at the City Cathedral Church to donate items of good quality that they would still wear to date. You inspire me to keep pushing myself as far as I can go. You spoke this book into existence! Thank You!

To my oldest daughter, Paryss. You were my first true love. You have been there with Mommy through everything, and I will forever love you for that. Mommy named her hair product line, "A Touch of Paryss," after you, and I will push hard to get them on the market. I love you.

To my only son, Tramell II. The love you show Mommy is a love like no other. Mommy is doing her best to raise you to be a perfect gentleman. I love you.

To my baby girl, Harper. You showed mommy how to love through pain. You, Tramell II, and Paryss are my strength. I love you.

To my granny Barbara and papa Larry. Words can't express how much I love and appreciate the both of you for all that you have done and are still doing.

To my parents, Joseph "Jojo" Hearne and Robbin Malone. I thank the both of you for blessing me with this thing called life. I thank the both of you for being awesome grandparents to my three babies. I love the both of you.

To my biological sisters and brothers—Courtnie, Jodeci, Raivyn, Joseph III, and Zamar. I love you all.

To my nephews, Baby Danny, Kaydon, and Joseph IV. Auntie loves you.

To A.D., you are a true inspiration, and very wise. If only you could share your wisdom and positivity, with the entire world. Thank you for reminding me to never stop dreaming. Thank you for your peaceful spirit. I appreciate you and your support!

To my grandma Bobbie Jean, granddaddy Greg, granny Verronica, papa Waymon, grandma Fed, papa Clark, papa Dave Roberts, granny Hatter, papa Hatter (R.I.P), the entire Hatter Family, granny Erma Taylor & family, aunt Jocelyn, aunt Stephanie Thompson, aunt Esther, uncle Alvin, aunt Renata, uncle Tracy, Treyvon, Tracie, Duanna Ann, Austin, Alesha Hooks(R.I.P), Trevin, Connie, Danielle, Domonique, uncle Carey & PK, Carey Jr. & Tonya, Brian & AJ, Regina, Jacob, Larry, Sharon & Tracy Conner, Chris, Kierra, baby Mitchell, Taura & Pamela Thrash, A.D., uncle Nick, aunt Angel, the Champ-JR, Tyson, Kerri, Ty Dillard, aunt Regina, uncle Thomas, uncle Walter, uncle Danny, Devante, aunt Geraldine, aunt Natalie, aunt Kimberly, Mama Mary, Ashley, Chris, Abby, aunt Tammy, aunt Sonia, uncle Jerry and the Brumfield family, aunt Valerie, Tierra, uncle Terrance, Terrance Jr. and the Cooper Family, Tasha, Toodie, Phylisia, Mark, Kendra, Tiffany, Schell, Tim, Jawntreice, Christian, Camryn, aunt Gladys, uncle Warren, granny Future Woodard & Leroy Woodard Sr.(R.I.P), aunt Gayle & the Woodard Family, Broderick, Billy "JR" Howard(R.I.P), aunt Chunte', uncle Will, the Hearne Family, the Malone Family, the Hurd Family, the Oliver Family, the Wilburn Family, aunt Stephanie, Darian, Monica & Lewis Family, aunt Jackie, uncle Chester, and the City Cathedral Church Family thank you for whatever purpose you've served in my life. I love you all.

To Derrick Stoner, thank you for being such a great friend. I appreciate you for being there for me through high school, college, and in our adult life! Congratulations to you and your beautiful wife La'Jatienne Stoner. I love the both of you!

To my superintendent, Fort Bend ISD Charles Dupre & Mrs. Dupre. Thank you!

To Cheryl Martin, you have the most beautiful spirit, and I appreciate all that you do. Hard work never goes unnoticed.

To Teresa Johnson, thank you for being you. You are truly a blessing to everyone you come into contact with.

To Trustee David & Sandra Peake. Thank you for giving me my first job in Corporate America.

To Doris Keener. Thank you for coaching me in baton twirling, through college. Thank you for your support through college.

To Professor Lee. Thank you for being the best band director in the land.

To Mary Brewster. Thank you for your support as my principal and for all that you do.

To Tracy Rich, you bring life to our campus and staff meetings. Thank you.

To James Kirk Patrick. I didn't know you while you were attending my karate belt ceremonies during my middle school years, but you are now one of my administrators. Thanks for all that you do.

To Candace Richmond. Thank you.

To Mrs. Bacon, as I always tell you, it doesn't matter whether you dress up, or dress down, you are always classy. I love that about you!

To Mrs. DeFlora-Johnson, your humor is one of a kind. Thank you!

To Mica Williams, Tiffany Olford, Tanea Booker-Brown. Thanks for your humor and support.

To Natalie Debboun. Thank you for being nice. You have a heart of gold.

To Mr. B. Thank You.

To Mrs. Raftie. Thank you for being a power coach. Thank you for all of your encouraging words.

To Cristine Smith thank you for your morning smiles!

To Juan Sosa & the custodial staff, thank you all for the late hours you work, to keep our school clean.

To Joselyn Coats & January thanks for all of the encouraging words.

To the sixth-grade math team—Ms. Budd, Mr. Strawder, Mr. Daniels, our math specialist, Ms. Turner and the entire math team. Thank you all for being so dependable.

To Ms. Baker, Thank you for your positivity.

To the Teacher of the Year committee in Fort Bend Independent School District. Thank you all for helping me jump-start this book by selecting me as a district finalist, and then as your District Teacher of the Year.

To all of my students, never stop dreaming! Believe and make your dreams come true!

To all educators. Thank you for your service and commitment to help change lives every day.

To Dr. Barbara Wilson, MD at Wilson Hand Surgery. Thank you for a successful surgery, and for all that you do. I am forever grateful.

To Oprah Winfrey, Ellen DeGeneres, Tyler Perry, and Steve Harvey. I pray that my book reaches you all someday, as you all continue to touch lives and inspire every day.

To all my readers. I pray that my book blesses your life in some way. "True knowledge will never expire, so share it!"

INTRODUCTION

EVERYTHING WENT BLACK as Musik Raine, everyone's favorite teacher, fell to the ground, clutching her stomach, praying to God that her unborn child was okay. Arguments led to her being slapped to the ground, choked until she blacked out, head bashed into doors and the floor on which she now lay. Blows to her face and chest left her breathless and in pain, scared to fight back out of fear of losing her babies. This was not the first time; neither was it the last. However, she noticed that each and every current situation prepared her for a future-present situation. It was all a part of growing up. Of course, she didn't plan for her life to go the way it did, but she figured it was all a part of the process. Musik made a choice not to waste her time on self-pity and sadness the day she realized that she was too big a gift to the world. So now, each day, the Lord blesses her with life, health, and strength. She is another step closer to her divine purpose, and she is forever grateful. She is humbled by struggle, is positively changed by pain, and is a success story in the making. Musik believes that the moment everyone realizes how to recover without hurting others, or one another, is the moment where they have finally grown up.

CHAPTER 1

Childhood Worries

GROWING UP, AT times, not even the sky is the limit. Dreaming big through daydreams and adolescent conversations with childhood friends becomes the everyday norm, while you, as a child, are expected to have no worries in the world. As a child, Musik began caring for people early and wanting to help in every way possible. The church was her favorite place, and she had the perfect plan to save the world. It was all so simple. Her plan was to get a big, huge van, to drive around the world to pick up all the homeless people, and then to take them to church. Why? Well, it's simple. Church fixed things and made everyone feel better. Church was a place of peace, away from all the troubles at home. School was another place of peace as she always strived to make all her teachers happy. They all seemed to have perfect lives, and the way they talked to her and to one another was different from the word choices expressed many days and nights within her household.

At one point, Musik's family was perfect. They lived in San Diego, California. Her family was made up of her father, Harp; her mother, Rose; her older sister, Harmony; her two younger sisters, Lyra and Demi; herself; and her younger brother, Quintus. The zoo, the movies, and on good nights, the bowling alley were places her family would go for family outings. These were all times that she had to cherish, because at any given time, things could take a turn for the worse. Let's just say, when things were good, it was best to live in the moment, because when things were bad, they were really bad. Parents, at times, can overlook the mere reality that children realize and remember all actions that come along with both positive and negative energy. As an adolescent, Musik could still remember Harmony and herself sitting in the back seat with their aunt Lyric while Harp and Rose argued to the point where things became physical. Physical slaps and punches were being passed back and forth and came to an end when Rose's head was bashed into a window, breaking the glass, and then came the blood.

They were in a drive-through at a fast-food restaurant. This behavior became a norm as the majority of Harp and Rose's arguments led to physical altercations. The worst of them all were nights where one or the other, or both Harp and Rose, would hold knives to each other's throats and then would yell for Harmony to call 911. Talking about mentally damaging, things only seemed to get worse. Musik, Harmony, Lyra, Demi, and Quintus were woken up from their sleep some nights due to Harp and Rose's arguments and physical altercations. When Harp and Rose fought, they fought to the point sometimes where the police had to get involved.

Musik grew very concerned late one night, when Rose had to be rushed to the emergency room. All Musik remembers from that night, was Rose walking out of the emergency room dragging her purse on the ground, without an ounce of energy left in her body. It was confirmed by physicians that Rose had a nervous breakdown. Another night, Harp had to be rushed to the emergency room, due to him having a stroke. Stress always makes and leaves a mess! So what does Musik think happened? Two hurting individuals married way too soon and ended up hurting each other for thirteen long years. They married before they lived and before they really knew who they were as individuals. This caused them to drive each other insane. Whether they were cursing each other out or physically fighting, they just couldn't seem to find a place of peace within their marriage, except for when they were being fruitful and multiplying.

Harp would spend long nights in the studio, trying to give the family a better life, but this left Rose stuck at home, tending to all five children, when she wasn't in the beauty salon, doing hair. Crazy thing is, Harp would have been able to give them a better life had it not been for selfish individuals messing over him. Musik was too young, at that point in time, for her opinion to matter, but if it was up to her, things would have been handled a lot differently. Musik remembers being in the studio with Harp on many days and nights as he produced music. Some artists used him and then dropped him after he put in all the groundwork. Believe it or not, all the secular artists paid. It was the gospel artists that messed him over. One gospel group is well-known and is still carrying on without a care in the world. Musik wondered for years why Harp never went after what was rightfully his, and even now, she still wonders.

CHAPTER 2

Hidden Secrets—Too Scared to Tell

There were some things Musik was just too young to understand. As a mother, it is okay to be deliberately protective. As a young girl, from time to time, Rose, while still married to Harp, allowed Musik to go to Ms. Darla's house. She was a friend of the family who lived across town. Ms. Darla had a son named Jameson, at the time, who was extremely nice to Musik, so she always enjoyed going to their house. It all came to an end one Sunday when Musik was left alone with Jameson while Ms. Darla made a store run. Musik had on a church dress with ruffles and, under her dress, a white slip. Before Ms. Darla left, she took Musik's dress off her, only leaving on her slip, in order for her to be comfortable.

Musik was in Jameson's room, sitting on his bed where she had been told to sit, while he sat on the floor playing his video game. All of a sudden, he paused his video game and instructed her to come lie on her back next to him. Musik was only six years old at the time. Before she knew it, Jameson began lifting up her slip and feeling and kissing all over her body. He kissed her on her cheek and then multiple times on her lips. He then put his hands in her underwear and began fondling her private area.

She was so terrified as he threatened to harm her if she was to say anything to anyone. As Jameson heard the front door opening, he quickly removed his hands from Musik's private area, pulled her slip down, and told her to hurry up and get back on his bed as he went back to playing his video game like nothing had happened. Ms. Darla came into his room to get Musik as she had been invited to attend a birthday party up the street, which was walking distance from their house. They never made it to the birthday party. As they began walking to the party, Musik did not know exactly how to explain what had just happened to her as she was still shook up.

She started off by telling Ms. Darla that Jameson had kissed her. Ms. Darla then asked her where, assuming that he had only kissed her on the cheek. Musik responded by telling her that he had kissed her on her lips and in other places. Musik then began crying and telling Ms. Darla everything else that Jameson did to her body. They immediately made a U-turn and headed straight back to the house.

All Musik could think of, at that time, was Rose telling her to tell someone if anyone touched her in a way that made her feel uncomfortable, so that's exactly what she did. When they arrived back at the house,

Ms. Darla went to Jameson's room to ask him what happened while she was at the store as she instructed Musik to gather her belongings. He pretended as if he did not know what she was asking him, and when she informed him of the things that Musik had mentioned to her as they were walking, he, of course, denied everything. As Musik and Ms. Darla got into her vehicle, she began yelling at Musik and telling her that she could never again come back to their house. She was yelling as if Musik had done something wrong. She tried to make it as if Musik was lying about her son, and at that moment, Musik wished that she hadn't said anything at all and just kept that situation to herself.

Ms. Darla made a phone call to Harp and Rose in order to inform them about the situation at hand and to also let them know that she was on her way to bring Musik home. When Musik arrived home, both Harp and Rose answered the door. Musik broke down crying again and expressed to both of her parents that she couldn't go back to Ms. Darla and Jameson's house anymore. She was so confused. As Musik and Ms. Darla walked in, Harp and Rose instructed her to go straight to her room. As she headed toward her room, she noticed that her family's living room was full of people. Harp; Rose; Grandmother Fay; Grandmother Ann; their two husbands, Larry and William; and a few people from the church were all gathered and were ready to meet about what had just taken place. Musik continued toward her room where Harmony, Lyra, and Demi were all standing by the door. As she entered, they all started asking her questions about what happened. Musik then told them that she could never go back to Jameson's house again because he had been kissing her.

It's funny how sexual encounters never leave one's memory bank, no matter how young they are. When Musik became old enough to understand the situation, she promised herself that if she was to ever have children, she would teach them how to help her protect them in situations like this. First off, she would inform them to fear no one, no matter how they try to threaten them. She would also stray away from giving their private areas nicknames. In this way, they could tell her exactly who touched, what was touched, and how it was touched. Ms. Darla was sure to keep her word as Musik never, ever again returned to her home.

CHAPTER 3

Breaking Point

A FEW YEARS PASSED, and Musik could never figure out why Rose hated the studio so much. She hated the studio to the point where she literally kicked the door off the hinges one night. Her argument was how Harp spent late nights at the studio and was still not bringing home what she felt was enough money to keep the household stable. Things had gotten bad, but it suddenly hit rock bottom on the sixth birthday of Musik's baby brother Quintus. It started off as a good night. Quintus was turning six, and Harp was taking the family bowling. This night in particular changed Musik's life for the rest of her life. She noticed that while they were bowling, Harp kept pacing back and forth while talking on his phone, close to where the restrooms were. Something just didn't feel right. All at once, the night ended early. Musik and her siblings were instructed to gather their belongings and to head back to the cars.

Musik, Harmony, Lyra, and Demi loaded into Rose's car while Quintus decided to get into Harp's van. Harp and Rose began to argue between their cars, which were parked parallel to each other. After yelling back and forth at each other, Rose stuck her head in the driver's side door of her car to tell Musik and her sisters that Harp had a baby from another woman. Musik wanted so bad for it to be a lie, so bad that she opened the door from the back seat and asked Harp if Rose was telling the truth. As Harp nodded his head yes, tears began to fall effortlessly from Musik's face. The back seat was full of tears as Musik and her sisters realized that their family was now over. Quintus was too young to understand any of this madness.

As Harp and Rose got into their own separate vehicles and drove off, Rose was so angry and not in her right mind that she began to chase behind Harp's van in an attempt to run him off the road. She continuously ran the front of her car into the back of his van until Musik reminded her that Quintus was in the car with him. The family made it safely to the house of Grandmother Fay—her dad's mother—where the arguing, fussing, and fighting continued.

Musik went mute, and out of anger and hurt, she wouldn't say a word. See, it was deeper than it seemed. Before this incident, Musik was a true daddy's girl. Everywhere Harp went, if she could go, she was there. Harp would pick Musik up from school, get her a Happy Meal from McDonald's, and then the both of them would go on to the studio where Musik would eat on the studio's floor as she watched her favorite cartoon, *Bobby's World*. See, she thought they had a bond, so how could Harp keep something like this from her? How could he do this to their family?

Anyways, at Grandmother Fay's house, Harp kept calling Musik's name for her to talk to him in the living room area, but she still refused to utter a word. As she walked out of her grandmother's house, he followed her enraged and then out of his mouth came, "You can't talk, so don't bring your motherfucking ass back to my house anymore." By that time, Grandmother Fay had come outside, and she told him that his word choice toward Musik, his own daughter, was uncalled for. Out of anger, Musik finally responded with "I hate you" and then ran and locked herself in Rose's car as Harp charged behind her and hit the window. The night seemed to get longer. Because the home of Musik's grandparents was disrupted, they had every right to send Musik and her family away. Harp and Rose carried on with everything but peace as they continued the conversation at a nearby gas station. More and more secrets that they had kept from each other surfaced, and all Musik and her siblings could do was listen and cry, praying for the night to end. Musik could not understand how two people who claimed to love each other could not only hurt each other so badly but also leave their kids hanging in the balance.

Christmases while Harp and Rose were married were the best, but this particular year, they could only afford to get Musik and her siblings one small used toy each, unwrapped. As far as a Christmas tree, there wasn't one, and it didn't feel like Christmas. Musik and her siblings never had the best of clothes. They never had the best of shoes. So they knew what it felt like to be less fortunate and to definitely not have what the other kids at school were blessed to have.

Of course, things continued to go downhill as Harp and Rose's marriage ended in divorce. Harp packed up and moved to Atlanta, Georgia, allowing Rose to keep all the kids as they took on the lifestyle of nomads. Musik's wonderful teachers at Destined for Greatness Elementary in Love Independent School District would all say that she hid her home life very well. The teachers in this district were professionals at capturing kids' hearts, which made it even harder to leave without being able to say goodbye.

Ms. Solomon had a huge impact on Musik's life. Ms. Solomon was her elementary school music teacher. She was responsible for teaching

Musik all fifty of the United States through song. She also helped Musik discover her love for singing. Musik may not be the best singer but she can definitely hold a note.

Ms. Letcher could make any student understand math. She was Harmony's math teacher, who Musik always wish she had. Ms. Letcher was so famous, that the students transformed her name into a song. They would sing, "*Oooh…Oooh…Ms. Letcher*" on the way to and from fieldtrips. She loved all of her students, and all of her students loved her back!

Mrs. Mosley, Musik's elementary librarian, introduced Musik to the American Girls. While in elementary, Musik was able to travel to Chicago, Illinois, with the American Girls Club, to the American Girl Place. Her favorite American Girl doll, was Aduke "Addy" Walker, an African American doll whose story books, Musik could relate to, and loved to read. Musik became homesick while in Chicago, but the trip turned out to be a blast. Grandmother Fay paid for her to go on the trip to Chicago, but during that time, she made it seem as if Musik's parents had paid for it. Grandmother Fay made up a lot of financial differences throughout the years, especially whenever her son Harp was short on bills.

Mrs. Smith, Musik's first-grade teacher, taught her handwriting and how to write in cursive. These were the only positive memories that Musik had to hold on to as her and her siblings packed up and moved away. Musik hid these memories deep in her heart.

After her parent's divorce, almost every three to six months, Musik and her siblings were being evicted and having to find somewhere else to live. Stability was nonexistent. Rose was doing the best she could now as a single parent of five kids, until men entered the equation. Whenever Musik came home from school and saw brown boxes, she already knew what time it was. Having to live in rodent- and insect-infected homes was no fun. Musik's and her siblings' clothes and shoes were food to the rodents. Rodents had no problem pissing and pooping on their clothes and shoes. They all wore hand-me-down clothes, so when their pants started to rise above their ankles, Musik would remove the hem to give their pants an extra inch. Then came the hot cigarette-smoke-filled motels and then trailers. Life only seemed to get worse.

Musik's mom now had a drug dealer of a boyfriend. His name was Mr. Dave, and he gave Musik bare-hand beatings to her body. That was not even the worst. Suffering many nights without lights or running water, bathing in buckets of store-bought water, and then attempting to complete her homework with a dull flashlight in a corner were Musik's day-to-day norms. Rose would always tell her and her siblings, "Don't y'all go talking our business to your granny Fay or nobody else . . . what goes on in this house, stays in this house." Musik tried to figure out what particular house she was referring to because they lived in quite a few.

CHAPTER 4

Silent Cries

MUSIK NEVER THOUGHT she could have so much hatred in her heart toward anyone, but her mom's boyfriend, Mr. Dave, was evil, inappropriate, and made all forms of hatred possible. He somehow always found a reason to physically whip her, not with a belt but with his bare hands. One night, while living in the trailer, Musik's little brother, Quintus, was swinging an umbrella and hit the sink. Mr. Dave came to the both of them from a small room in the back of the trailer where he and Rose were and asked what happened. Quintus admitted that it was him who had swung the umbrella and hit the sink, but with his bare hands to Musik's butt, Mr. Dave hit her continuously until he felt like he was tired. The trailer was compact, so Musik knew that Rose wasn't asleep because she had just heard her talking to Mr. Dave right before he came out of their small room in the back. The room's door was wide open, so Rose witnessed the entire situation. Musik looked at Rose in the eyes and asked her why she was just letting this man hit her like that. Rose pretended to be asleep until Musik mentioned that she was going to tell Harp. That obviously pressed a button because Rose immediately jumped up, got in Musik's face as if she was a random person off the street, and then told Musik that if she and her siblings were to get split up or taken away, the blame would be on her. Musik believed those words for years.

Another time, Musik was left at home by herself, at another residence, with Mr. Dave, and Rose was nowhere to be found. Musik was in her room, attempting to do her homework, when Mr. Dave yelled her name once, as if something was wrong. When she came to where he was, he started striking her with his hand extremely hard on her back and butt, and for the first time, he picked up a belt and began hitting her even harder. Musik was finally able to grab the belt to stop Mr. Dave from hitting her as she yelled at him and told him that he was not her daddy. When he stopped hitting her, she ran to a corner in her room and just cried. She had no cell phone, and he wouldn't give her the house phone to call someone. He kept pacing back and forth in front of her room door. Musik was so terrified. Mr. Dave lied to Rose and told her that he whipped Musik because he kept calling her and she was ignoring him when he had honestly, only called Musik's name once. He was only looking for a reason to whip her. Musik assumed that Mr. Dave must have been using some of the drugs that he was selling.

All of a sudden, there was a knock at the front door. Because it was late at night, Musik assumed that it was just drug addicts coming to buy drugs. There was a long sheet in front of the hallway opening to block Musik and her siblings, when the drug addicts were there, from seeing any drug activity that transpired during nighttime. By the grace of God, the knock on the door was Grandmother Ann—the mother of Rose, who came to pick up Musik for the night.

No matter what, Rose always took Mr. Dave's side. Musik noticed that, out of all her sisters, she could never dress comfortable. She was told not to wear shorts and other clothing items. Rose made her wear too-big, long cotton pants and too-big T-shirts in front of Mr. Dave. Soon Musik found out the reasoning behind it one day while Rose was doing her hair. While Rose stared at Musik in a mirror with an evil look on her face, she said to her, "I know you like my man, but all that you're doing, you better stop." Every word was a deeper stab to Musik's heart as tears formed and just fell. Musik was still a child and couldn't believe that Rose thought that she wanted Mr. Dave. It was sickening! Musik was only in middle school at the time. As she immediately stopped Rose from doing her hair, Rose leaned in close to Musik's ear and whispered, telling her that she better not tell anyone. Mr. Dave stared from a distance, with an evil smirk on his face.

A few weeks later, Musik came home from school and saw brown boxes. They were being evicted from that particular residence and had to go live in a hot, sweaty, smoke-filled motel room with roaches and one raggedy mattress that God knows how many sexual partners had been on it. That motel room was so unsanitary. If Musik could have just floated in the air to keep from touching anything in that room, she would have, but even the air was unsanitary. Even here, Rose made Musik put on those too-big, long cotton pants and too-big T-shirts.

It was sweat-dripping hot in this motel room, and Rose took it a step further by making Musik lie down in the nasty bed in a specific way and then that evil look of hers came out again as she made Musik get under the thick cover, covering up her entire body. Rose laid on the floor with Mr. Dave. When Musik's other sisters asked to go elsewhere during times like this, they were able to, but no matter how many times Musik begged to go stay with one of her grandmothers, Mr. Dave would intervene and tell Rose that Musik needed to stay home. Mr. Dave won, and Musik had to stay home.

Years later, when Mr. Dave and Rose finally broke up, Musik mentioned to Rose's two sisters, Paige and Sasha, a few of the situations that had taken place because she was holding so much in. Musik even mentioned to them the incident of Rose thinking that she wanted Mr. Dave. They were both infuriated. Come to find out, Musik wasn't the issue. Rose knew all along that it was Mr. Dave looking at Musik in a sexual way, but still, that was not enough for her to let him go. She chose him.

Because of him, Musik had even given up on being able to celebrate the day she was born. Her birthday was special to her once upon a time—when her biological parents, Harp and Rose, were married—because she and Harp shared the same birthday—twenty years apart. However, after their divorce, Musik was told by Rose that her birthday was just another day. The funny thing was, when Musik's birthday rolled around, Rose had no money to celebrate, but there was always money for her other siblings when their birthdays rolled around. It was also funny because Mr. Dave's birthday was not too far from Musik's birthday. (We're talking about a two- to three-day difference.) And while she received nothing due to her mom not having any money, a few days later for Mr. Dave's birthday, Rose purchased him a card, balloons, clothes, etc. Musik just accepted all that was going on because it was out of her control.

CHAPTER 5

Escape

WHILE STILL IN middle school, Musik discovered her passion for baton twirling and marched in the band for the first time at Hope Middle School in Study Hills Independent School District. Her band director at the time, Mr. Penson, was responsible for teaching her that, in band, she was always supposed to start marching on her left foot. This stuck with Musik for her entire band career. She finally started to feel like a normal kid as she was able to twirl at pep rallies, at football games, and march in parades. Baton twirling did something for Musik, and when she finally got the concept of tossing and catching the baton with the same hand, it became the best way for Musik to relieve stress.

While at Hope Middle School, Grandmother Fay paid for Musik to go on a camping trip in Arkansas. Grandmother Fay also purchased everything Musik needed for camp, in terms of new clothes, shoes, socks, underwear, swimsuits, towels, soap, shampoo, conditioner, and so forth. The name of the camp was, *Camp Ozark*. One of Musik's sixth grade teachers—Ms. Sarafin, sent Musik and two other students who were excelling academically, to this six-week Christian camp. While at camp, Ms. Sarafin wrote Musik and the other two students once a week. Attending this particular camp was a great experience for Musik.

Musik and Harmony both twirled before there was an actual band at Hope Middle School. So they would go to the games and just twirl to music that was played from a radio in the stands. Somehow the baton and Harmony's hands couldn't find a common ground or meeting place. Of course, at games, Harmony would wait until it was extremely quiet and then down the stands her baton went, metal to metal, hitting every metal row in the stands on the way down. The look on Harmony's face, would be priceless, as her baton made its way down the stands. Life at home still wasn't on the up and up, but it no longer mattered because Musik had finally tapped into something that made her happy.

Musik was also a part of the Chuck Norris Kickstart program, with the best karate instructor, Mr. Gangloff. Sparring Fridays were her favorites because she was able to put on gloves and other sparring equipment and box with both boys and girls. Belt ceremonies made her feel valued, just like at the A-B Honor Roll Award Assemblies. She still had unfinished business in that area though because, once she graduated, she stopped at red belt and never knew that she could go back to continue training for her black belt.

Being a part of Kickstart taught Musik discipline and self-control. Being a part of the band gave her another way to replace negative energy with positive vibes. Musik was thankful for a great team of teachers, from elementary through college, that had an impact on her life. They included but are not limited to Coach Baker-"The Dodge-Ball Champ", Mrs. Herman, Mrs. Smith, Ms. Ward, Ms. Letcher, Mrs. Constance Jackson, Ms. Braxton, Mrs. Solomon-Keys-Terry, Mrs. Balque, Ms. Sarafin, Ms. Campbell, Mr. Cain, Mr. Myers, Mr. Boyd, Mr. Davis, Mr. Ioda, Mrs. Davis, Mr. Shelton, Mr. Penson, Mr. Joseph, Mr. Falco, Chief Bradford, Professor Singleton, Professor Lee, Professor Gipson, Professor Johnson, and Professor Franklin. She was also grateful for her baton twirling coaches—Mrs. Grear, who was a sixth-grade principal, and the first to put a baton in her hand, Ms. Webber, Ms. Blair, and Mrs. Keener.

CHAPTER 6

Attempt to Fill a Void

HIGH SCHOOL WAS a pretty interesting journey. Musik completed ninth grade at the Criminal Justice High School, tenth grade and eleventh grade at Carmen Vanguard High School, and twelfth grade at Cheraé High School. Rose had a rule that Musik and her sisters couldn't date until their senior year of high school. They kind of stuck to it, but . . . well . . . moving on.

Musik tried out for the baton twirling team at Cheraé High School during the end of her freshman year at the Criminal Justice High School. She made the team, but Rose wouldn't allow her to go to Cheraé High School just yet. So her only other option was to attend high school with Harmony at Carmen Vanguard High School. This particular high school was straight academic and had no sports, so this allowed Musik to leave school early to take her last class period of the day at Cheraé, which was band. Weekly football games and weekend parades were so exciting. Halftime shows and dancing in the stands were Musik's high.

The only time reality hit Musik was at football games when she would look into the stands before a halftime performance and not see either one of her parents. She appreciated the few games that Grandmother Fay and Papa Larry came to. At the same time, she could only remember her parents coming to support her at only one to two football games during her high school years. Of course, it bothered her because the majority of the band members and auxiliary girls had their family there to support them for almost every single performance. She eventually adjusted and tried not to let it bother her as much.

Musik met her first love and experienced her first heartbreak during her high school years. She found a videotape of her first love having sex with a girl who was supposed to be her friend. Other issues of that sort included but were not limited to phone texts and e-mails. Musik's first love was older than her and more experienced, but the most important thing to her was how he was somehow filling a void. The fact that he was the first guy that she trusted, after Harp let her down, caused the hurt to penetrate even deeper. This was a situation that she wished was "he say, she say" because actually seeing it with her own eyes really did hurt. Everything that she cherished, everything they did, was no longer special because the same love he shared with Musik, was shared with another girl. However, she guessed that's what she got for asking God to show her the truth, no matter how bad it would hurt. He did just that.

Musik did have a childhood boyfriend, but the most they ever did was hang out and kiss a few times, nothing more. They were really young. At the start of high school, he broke up with her because another girl that he was talking to was giving him more than Musik was. Long distance had never been an issue before, but all of a sudden, it became an issue. He wanted to be free, so Musik allowed him to fly away. She just wasn't ready. High school didn't make her ready either, but she figured that she was searching for love in all the wrong places.

Musik never knew how badly she needed her father until he wasn't there when she needed him the most. She needed him there to teach and show her how guys were supposed to treat her. How was she supposed to act on a date? How was the guy supposed to treat her on a date? How was she supposed to handle her first heartbreak? What was she supposed to do to get over her heartbreak period? She needed him to teach her how to set standards and to simply tell her the truth about boys. Every girl needs her father throughout her life—in some areas more than others. No one or nothing can replace that need.

She finally got over her first love and met a real handsome fellow named Ramon at a church revival. Boy, was he handsome and in really good shape. Everything about him wasn't perfect, but his best features, Musik would have to say, were his smile and that crazy laugh of his. He was Musik's first *official* boyfriend, in terms of when Rose actually allowed her to date and have a boyfriend. Musik didn't have to hide him.

Their relationship became complicated one Friday when Musik received a phone call from him telling her that he was in jail. Her heart skipped a beat. She asked him what happened and when he was getting out; however, he couldn't go into details. Musik planned on being there for him every step of the way until his baby sister came to her and relayed a message from him telling Musik not to wait on him. Musik wanted to hear it from him herself. When Ramon received his sentence, it took Musik's breath away, but she was still up for the challenge. Everyone around Musik was calling her dumb for waiting and holding him down while he was in jail. But she ignored them, and she was there for him the best way she knew how.

Musik's father, Harp, was still in Atlanta, and he reached out to her when he found out that she was holding this guy down while he was in jail. The two of them began to argue back and forth until Harp mentioned a girl's name, asking Musik who the girl was, and then telling her that Ramon was playing her. At this point, she really didn't want to hear what Harp had to say because, in her mind, he had just up and left her and their family. However, if Musik knew then what she knew now, she would have listened because Harp obviously saw extreme hurt coming from this situation long before it surfaced. Of course, being young and naive, Musik didn't want to believe it, but she still wanted to know whether or not the allegations were true. So she wrote a letter to Ramon in jail, asking him who the girl was, and she asked him to come clean about whatever he was hiding from her. He wrote her back and came clean, admitting to her that he was playing her and with not only that particular girl. He had also been writing to a good number of other females, telling them what they wanted to hear. After that letter, Musik decided to let him go, and she didn't respond to any more letters that he sent. Sometimes, when letters came in, she wouldn't even open them. She threw a few of them away out of anger. He straight up played her and was never real with her to begin with. She moved on with her life in hopes to never look back.

Trusting the wrong people will have one headed for disaster every single time. Musik tried her best to guard her heart, but it was extremely difficult because when she loved, she loved hard. If she was in a relationship with anyone, it was only them and no one else. This heartbreak was what made Musik realize that she needed Harp. She was hurt, lost, and she needed him badly. She ended up heartbroken when attempting to fill a void that he once filled. Harp was in no form or fashion responsible for Musik's heartbreaks or hurt. She made her own decisions, and for that reason, she had to live with each and every one of them. She just wished that she had his guidance, from the viewpoint of a man.

Meanwhile, at her current residence, Harmony and Musik had to become parents to Lyra, Demi, and Quintus as Rose went out of town for a period of three to six months to make enough money to catch up on bills. Musik didn't know what Rose worked out with the landlord at the time, but the bills were paid up this time. Grandmother Ann and Papa William—the parents of Rose—helped out as much as they could and would stop by from time to time to check on Musik and her other siblings. Harmony and Musik had to make sure that their younger siblings ate, which was frozen food from the freezer, and also had to make sure they were up and ready for school. Harmony didn't have her license yet, but she drove their younger siblings and Musik to school in what they called the Scooby Doo Mystery Van. Musik prayed the entire way—to and from school—because at the time, let's just say, Harmony wasn't a professional driver. But she did get them to where they needed to be. God looked out for them, and they never got pulled over by the police.

CHAPTER 7

The Fight

DURING MUSIK'S SENIOR year in high school, she had the greatest best friend in the world. They were in the band together at Cheraé High School. His name was Dedrick. He faithfully picked Musik up from where she was living at the time and allowed her to ride to school with him every single day. He also dropped her off at home after band practice. She could talk to him about anything and get sound advice, and in the event that she was wrong, he had no problem telling her that she was!

He started teaching her how to drive on her street. As she became a little bit more comfortable driving, he allowed her to drive to school. However, because she wasn't a professional, one of their friends Kendal, who Dedrick also picked up in the mornings, would nearly be about to have a heart attack while she was driving, so Dedrick would just go ahead and drive. Musik and Dedrick's favorite song was *"What a Job"* by Devin the Dude.

One day she was about to start driving on the wrong side of the street, but before pulling out of a neighborhood, he told her to stop and to put the car in park. They just sat there, and then he told her to just sit quietly and watch as people drove by. The people driving by looked at Musik crazily for being on the wrong side of the street. She never attempted to drive on the wrong side of the street again. Another time while driving, he yelled at Musik and said, "Friend, never switch lanes in an intersection." She never switched lanes in an intersection again.

They ended up going to separate colleges. While still in high school, Dedrick was the only person that Musik could trust and talk to about her personal problems, even about the issues that she and Rose had. He listened and never judged her.

During Musik's senior year in high school, she flew to Atlanta— where Harp was— and tried out to be a feature twirler at Barack Obama University (BOU). She made it and received a baton-twirling scholarship. Musik thanked her high school band director—Mr. Joseph— for opening the door for her to consider joining the band at Barack Obama University. His support of her through high school was remarkable. Cheraé High School paid for the entire band one year, including auxiliary, to attend the band's Power Camp during the summer at BOU. This, along with consistent practice, was what really prepared Musik to be a collegiate feature twirler. She flew back home after tryouts.

Ever since Rose thought that Musik wanted Mr. Dave, their relationship was nonexistent. Musik avoided her as much as possible. For years, Rose complained about the little to none child support that she was receiving from Harp. Musik really wasn't concerned because she and her siblings never saw any of it. Rose and Harmony literally fought all the way into the streets before Harmony moved out. Musik did what she could to pull Rose off Harmony the best way she knew how. It was now time for Musik to go off to college, and she too had to fight.

Musik never would have imagined herself getting into a physical altercation with her own mother. She remembered sitting on her bed, at yet another residence, three days before *Band Camp* at BOU. It was actually the house that Musik and her siblings grew up in before Harp and Rose's divorce. Rose was sitting at her computer desk and started complaining to Musik about what Harp wasn't doing, which was her normal routine. Musik was tired of hearing it, so she told Rose that she didn't care and didn't feel like hearing it. She was just trying to pack and leave for college in peace. Rose then threatened Musik by telling her that she would burst her head open and then beat her until meat shows. Musik responded by telling Rose that if she did that, she would go to jail. Rose immediately got up from her computer desk and charged into Musik's room, getting in her face and poking her in her face and forehead with her nails, asking Musik what she was going to do, while getting into a fighting stance.

While Rose was talking, spit from her mouth was landing on Musik's face. Musik told her that she could hear her and then informed her that she was spitting in her face. Rose then responded, nonchalantly, by telling Musik that if she spits on her, she was just spit on. She went back to poking Musik in the face and forehead with her nails.

All of a sudden, Musik blanked out, grabbed a pair of jeans off her bed that hadn't been packed yet, and swatted Rose with them. Rose roughly started pulling out Musik's real hair and punching Musik in the head with her fist. She pulled out patches of Musik's real hair! To make Rose release her hair, Musik pushed her as hard as she could into the wall by her bedroom window. Musik's bedroom door was cracked, and as Rose pushed her back, the crease of Musik's back hit the door itself. Musik fell to the ground, and before she knew it, Rose had picked up one of Musik's metal baton sticks and began hitting her with it. As Rose stood over her, she lost count of how many times Rose hit her with the metal baton stick. Musik had bruises all down her arms, between her legs, and a swollen and fractured wrist covered in blood splats. Her scalp was knotted up and was bleeding from where Rose had pulled her hair out. Musik's two younger sisters, Lyra and Demi, walked in while Rose was striking her with the baton and just stood there. Musik remembered looking up at them and yelling, "So y'all are just going to watch and not help me stop her from hitting me with this baton?" If the shoe was on the other foot, Musik would have stopped Rose from abusing them, especially if there was a metal stick involved. She knew that if Harmony was there, she would have had her back, the same way Musik had her back when Rose jumped on her before she moved out. One time, Rose spanked Musik with the cord, of an *Old-School* remote control, but Musik never would have imagined Rose beating her with a metal stick.

Musik's Aunt Paige called her the next day and came with her cousin Laila to come pick her up and to take her shopping for college clothes. Paige was proud of Musik for going to college and knew a few of the struggles she and her other siblings had to endure. Musik wore jeans, which hurt to put on, and she covered the bruises on her arms with a jacket. It was summertime, and it was over eighty degrees outside, so her aunt and cousin looked at her as if she was crazy. As far as her fractured wrist, she considered herself blessed because had she not lifted her wrist to cover her head while Rose was beating her with the baton, her head would have received the strike that was powerful enough to fracture her wrist.

While shopping, Musik and Laila ended up sharing the same dressing room while trying on clothes. As time passed, Musik forgot about the bruises that she was attempting to hide. Musik and Laila were having a normal conversation, and then, all of a sudden, Laila stopped responding. Laila immediately asked Musik what happened. Musik burst into tears and couldn't answer, so Laila's next question was whether or not Rose did it. Musik nodded her head yes, and Laila, in return, called Paige into the dressing room. Laila explained to Paige what was going on, as Paige took a look at all of Musik's bruises and her fractured wrist. She grew very angry. Musik begged both Laila and her aunt Paige not to mention anything. Musik just wanted to assure that she got out of that house safely and without another fight. Paige informed Musik's other aunt, Sasha, and they both informed

Grandmother Ann. They all called to check on Musik. Harmony also called to check on Musik, when she found out about the incident. It got back to Rose, and she picked another fight. Rose was actually proud of what she had done and was bragging about the fact that she beat Musik with her own baton stick. Rose would say things like "I surely did, and I'll do it again." This time, Musik didn't fight her back, but instead, she chose to ignore her and attempted to walk out of the house. When she realized that leaving was impossible, due to Rose blocking the door, she went to her room and waited for sunrise.

The third day after the fight, Papa William—the father of Rose—came to pick Musik and her belongings up and drove her to the airport. She caught the first flight to Atlanta, heading to Barack Obama University. It took Musik and Papa William thirty minutes flat to load up and head to the airport. When they drove off, Musik never looked back. She ignored Rose's calls and, eventually, ended up blocking her from her phone as Rose was leaving her long, dramatic voicemails about Musik ignoring her phone calls. Musik didn't communicate with Rose for almost nine months.

Musik tried to make sense out of Rose fracturing her wrist, knowing that she needed both of her wrists to twirl in college band. Musik's Aunt Sasha flew up to Atlanta, with her uncle Ken, to wrap Musik's wrist the night before her first day of *Band Camp*. For the first few weeks of *Band Camp*, she wore long black tights and a long-sleeved shirt under her band T-shirt in ninety-plus-degree weather, to cover her bruises.

Musik flew from Atlanta back home to San Diego, California, to visit and to attend a family gathering months later. Rose was at the family gathering and found it humorous to spark a conversation and made a joke in front of the entire family, laughing and asking the family if anyone had ever been beaten with their own baton sticks. She, of course, was making reference to the fight between Musik and Rose. The family all looked at Rose like she was crazy as the majority of them expressed to her that nothing was funny about that incident. Musik never imagined having so much hatred in her heart, especially toward her own mother. God and prayer for months at a time kept Musik sane and helped her learn how to forgive Rose.

CHAPTER 8

College Life and One Life Loss

MUSIK'S FIRST YEAR of college was different. She was in a college band and participated in her first President Classic as a now-collegiate feature twirler. The President Classic was the big football game between Barack Obama University and Chicago Town State University. Late-night band practices, early-morning classes, and midday pep rallies were all good times. Traveling to out-of-state games was exciting, and this allowed Musik to legally skip a few classes.

One Valentine's Day, a tall, nice-looking, chocolate man named Tyrese approached Musik's doorstep with a fake rose, asking her to be his valentine. They lived in the same apartments, and he was the best barber on BOU's campus. Musik had never been out on a real date, so this was interesting. She accepted his invite, and eventually, he became her boyfriend. He was also a good cook—something that she really struggled with at the time. Let's just say, she made some gravy once, and it looked like oatmeal. They had good times but were still young. He, like the others, lied and cheated. He even went to the extent one night of telling Musik that a girl sent him some pictures of herself in a bra and panties for one of his homeboys. Musik asked him whether or not it looked like she had stupid written on her forehead. Tyrese and Musik argued about the situation and then moved past it.

As months passed by, Musik had finally started working her first little job. Jesse Hill High School was in the same area as where they were living at the time, so she would walk there to teach a baton twirling class for an after-school program. The hotter the temperature got outside, the longer the walks seemed, so on some days, she asked Tyrese for rides to work. His dropping her off to work became an issue, and it wasn't even every day that he had to drop her off to work. So she just stopped asking him. Funny thing was, one day he told her that he couldn't take her to work. That same day, he made time to take one of his homegirls to work and to pick her up, and whenever that girl needed him to do so, he came through. So Musik figured that she was no longer a priority to him. Musik even offered him gas money. When it came to men, Musik sure did know how to pick them.

Months later, Musik's Papa Larry allowed her to take over the notes on one of his cars and had it transported to where she was in Atlanta. So she now had her own vehicle. She started another job at a trustee's office that paid more money than the other job in which she was able to afford the car notes. She would go to class early in the mornings, would get off and go to work at the trustee's office for the second half of the day, and then would go to band practice. Her days were extremely long. On some days, when she left the trustee's office, she still had time to go and teach the baton-twirling class at Jesse Hill High School, right before band practice.

The relationship with Tyrese taught Musik how to be tough, not because of what they went through but because of how they ended. She asked him once why he changed and was no longer doing the things that he had once done to get her. His response was one that stuck with Musik for a lifetime. His response was "I no longer have to do those things because I have you already. It's like working for a championship ring that you already have!"

Musik had become pregnant and was going into her second trimester when things suddenly took a turn for the worse. She was at work, in front of her desk, and her body became extremely hot. She was not feeling well at all. Her stomach began to hurt extremely bad to the point where she felt like she was being stabbed. She immediately went to her supervisor's office and told her that she needed to go home. Her supervisor looked at her and told her that her face looked flushed and that she did not look well. She gave the okay for Musik to go home for the day. Musik then felt like she had to use the restroom, not number one but number two. Sorry . . . that was too much information, but it is what it is.

As she began using the restroom, it turned out that she did not have to defecate, but instead, two huge blood clots left her body and fell into the toilet. As she walked out of the restroom and proceeded to her vehicle, one of her coworkers, Charlize, who had become one of her close friends, followed her down the stairs to her car. In pain, Musik fell to the ground, clutching her stomach. This was her first pregnancy, so she had no idea what was going on with her body. She was getting ready to drive herself to the hospital, but it was impossible.

Charlize called Musik's dad, who wasn't too far away, to come get her and take her to the emergency room. The pain only seemed to get worse. Musik's supervisor came downstairs to where they were and told Charlize to just go ahead and call an ambulance to come and get Musik. When the ambulance finally arrived, the nurses strapped Musik to the stretcher and rushed her to the hospital. She began coughing and throwing up. The more she coughed, the more blood came out of her body. Thank the Lord she had on dark-brown pants. When she arrived at the hospital, they confirmed that she was indeed dilating and miscarrying.

The doctor grabbed clamps in order to pull her baby out as he or she was not completely formed. When the doctor pulled the baby out, Musik raised herself up to see the baby as the doctor laid him or her on the bed. The doctor made Musik lie back down and started to suction the baby's remains out of her body.

Now, before the ambulance pulled off from their job, Charlize had also called Tyrese, as they were also close friends, to let him know that Musik was on the way to the hospital. Tyrese told Charlize that he could not leave work and did not show up until everything was over.

The doctor sent Musik home with a pill to finish cleaning out her body. Tyrese drove her home when they discharged her from the hospital. That same night, he broke up with her, telling her that he wasn't happy. It just wasn't meant to be.

After the loss and with so much going on, Musik didn't know how to accept everything that had just taken place. She did know, however, that she felt so alone. She went into a depression but managed to push through. Tattoos somehow eased her pain. Every time she would hurt behind any situation, tattoos somehow, at this point in her life, eased the pain. She fell in love with body art. She just had to make sure that all her tattoos were able to be covered up when she put on her baton-twirling uniforms, in the event that she was to tryout for the marching band again.

Football season rolled around again, and Musik did decide to try out again for the band. Every year, auxiliary girls had to tryout, no matter how good they were. The band was her life, and because she was able to release so much stress by simply tossing up her batons, the football field became her paradise. The adrenaline rush that came right before she would hit the field for the halftime show was something serious!

CHAPTER 9

Sisterhood

WHILE IN THE band, Musik noticed a phenomenal group of women who were committed to serving the band. They fed the band members and provided them with water and Gatorade at the games. They helped pass out uniforms to the instrumentalists in the band, and they did so much more. Even more so, the love they showed toward one another was deeper than any bond Musik was familiar with. She knew that she had to become a part of their sisterhood. From their chapter song to their stepping and loyalty to the band, this was the perfect organization for her.

A group of seven other band girls and Musik decided to join. Becoming a part of the Tau Beta Sigma National Honorary Band Sorority helped Musik define the true meaning of sisterhood. Her line sisters—Keara, Angie, Arnecia, Alexus, Patricia, Rolicia, Daphne—and herself formed an even stronger bond and were overjoyed to now take part in helping serve the band under the direction of Mr. Lee. Musik appreciated Mrs. Hunter, who was a motherly figure to almost every band member and a beautiful inspiration to her.

Musik's line number was number 4, and her "big sister" name was Luv-TAU-Twirl. However, to the band, she was and will always be Twirler Girl. Mr. Lee, her band director, shocked her one night as he called her by that name and had her to end band practice that night with a prayer, as they had done every single night, but with a different band member.

Two years later, Musik joined another sorority named, Alpha Kappa Alpha Sorority Incorporated. This particular sorority was what she had dreamed about becoming a part of since the sixth grade. Her sixth-grade English teacher, Mr. Davis, taught her the Greek alphabet and told her that she would be an AKA one day. She joined their sisterhood in spring 2011. Musik's prophyte, Shy, was her big sister in this particular sorority, and gave Musik her "big sister" name. Musik's line number was number 5, and her "big sister" name was Motion PiKture. Her line sisters—Ashley, Emerald, Latricia, Evelyn, Kayla, Ariana, Mandy, Sharhonda, Jasmine, Dior, Raphy, Deshara, Antoiniece, Alicia, and Serena—also formed a bond.

To Musik, these two organizations were, indeed, the best of both worlds. One was considered a Greek organization and the other non-Greek. Both of these organizations are full of phenomenal women worldwide. If Musik had to do it all over again, she would choose the same two organizations. Both organizations, along with other life experiences, made her a better woman. Tau Beta Sigma- "For Greater Bands" …Alpha Kappa Alpha- "Service to all Mankind."

CHAPTER 10

First Real Love

AN UNEXPLAINABLE LOVE filled Musik's heart when she gave birth to her first child. He was so handsome. Musik named him England. When she held him in her arms, she finally realized what it felt like to truly love and to be truly loved back. Looking into England's eyes let Musik know that everything was going to be all right. Musik was now a mother, and she wanted to be the best mother possible. She was still in school at the time—her last year of college to be exact, and had her own apartment.

Musik worked and went to class up until the day it was time for her to give birth to England and then returned back to class two weeks after giving birth to him. His father, Reed, was not there to witness his birth as Musik had found out a dark secret when she was seven months pregnant.

Musik and Reed met on a band trip in Mississippi and started hanging out from there. When Musik met him, his story was that he was involved with someone, but it wasn't that serious. She should have walked away, but she didn't. Reed was a good friend and a great listener. He was fun to be around and good looking. They made decisions, and things happened. Musik took full responsibility for her decision not to walk away.

Reed would bring Musik lunch and food all the time during her pregnancy, whenever she had breaks from class. He even gave her a bank card to save money for their son; however, Musik never used it. Things between them came to an end one night while Musik was laying on her couch in her apartment during the seventh month of her pregnancy. Musik received a call from Reed. He told her that she was going to be mad at him, and then that's when he dropped the bomb that he was married and had been. He was planning for a big wedding. Musik didn't know what to say, but she grew very angry and just hung the phone up in his face. She cried for the rest of the night, but that's the price she had to pay for not walking away before anything had transpired between the two of them. Musik spoke with his wife and identified with her hurt and pain. She heard the same pain in her voice that she heard in Rose's voice when she found out that Harp had a baby from another woman.

After Musik found out that Reed was married, they never messed around, in any way, ever again. He wasn't there for England's birth, but when they were discharged from the hospital, he contacted Musik to ask if he could come and see the baby.

Musik didn't go to her apartment when she was discharged, however, she stayed with her close friend and coworker, Charlize, who supported her after she gave birth to England, and until she returned back to her own apartment. Reed came to the house of Charlize to see England and brought him a pack of diapers. Musik asked him if his wife knew that he was coming by, but he didn't respond. Musik and Reed were completely done with each other, but whatever the two of them had gone through, had nothing to do with their son. As of now, Reed is active in England's life and has been since England was one year old.

Musik still managed to graduate college on time. She graduated from Barack Obama University, in the winter, with her bachelor's degree in administration of justice. She was truly grateful for Grandmother Fay and Papa Larry because when she couldn't count on anyone else, they were there. They actually packed up and relocated to Atlanta for a few months to help out with England so that Musik was able to finish school and her last year of the four years that she had promised to the band. Many days, when she fell short on money, they would come through, and thank the Lord for Papa Larry keeping her gas tank full. Grandmother Fay helped Musik make sense out of many situations. She would always say, "You are not the first woman to be made a fool out of, and you are not going to be the last . . . so let God deal with them while you move on." Right will always win in the end.

CHAPTER 11

Behind Most Smiles

ANOTHER CHAPTER OF Musik's life began when her first official boyfriend, Ramon, came home from prison. Somehow they managed to get back in touch with each other, and agreed to remain friends. Musik started back writing letters to him and putting money on his books—commissary, until he came home. When Ramon finally came home, he borrowed money, flew to Atlanta to visit Musik and was introduced to England, who he had only seen in pictures and knew of through letters. He decided to stay in Atlanta, and the two of them ended up reconciling.

Musik and Ramon did a series of making up and breaking up. By this time, Musik's grandparents had returned back to their home, in California, and Ramon had moved in with Musik. Because of his criminal record, Ramon was unable to get any residence in his name. Musik took on a second job to support the family until Ramon found a job. Musik redid Ramon's resume, helped him obtain his driver's license through an online course that she paid for, and supported him the best way she knew how until things got better.

Two years later, Musik ended up pregnant by Ramon with a baby girl and decided to move back home to California, where the majority of both of their families were and where she began her teacher certification program. Here is where Musik was offered her first teaching position. The two of them moved into another apartment, but of course, it had to go in Musik's name because of Ramon's record. He soon began using the fact that his name wasn't on the lease as an excuse to why he didn't consistently help out with rent and the other bills.

Musik began teaching high school math at Victory High School, at a charter school in California. By this time, Ramon had become very physically abusive as time passed. Musik took responsibility for the first time Ramon hit her. Ramon was dropping Musik off to work in her car, and she snatched his phone when she saw a message from one of his ex-girlfriends that he had recently cheated on her with, pop up. He then slapped Musik hard in the face. She hit him back, and before she knew it, he had bashed her head into the passenger-side window—the same exact way that she witnessed Harp bashing Rose's head into the passenger-side window when she was younger.

After months of searching and going on interviews, Ramon finally found a job. Musik was so happy for him because she knew how hard it was for him to find a job with his record and knew that, because she had been carrying the load for so long, he would start helping out. For months, she had paid the rent, electricity, and water all by herself, including daycare and the prenatal doctor appointments. So any type of relief would have been helpful. Ramon was so excited when he received his first check, and helping with bills wasn't in any of his plans. Musik asked him if he could at least help her pay for half of the next doctor visit, and he responded to her by asking her what she would do if he never got the job.

Boy, did he teach her a lesson really quick with those few words. After all she had done for him. She felt so dumb! She was pregnant, getting dropped off to work in her own car, and catching rides home with coworkers while he drove her car to his job. If Musik didn't need the money, she wouldn't have asked for it. Ramon wanted to enjoy his first check, but Musik had two jobs and never enjoyed a single check.

During the next doctor's appointment, Ramon came along to support and was on the phone with his mother, Kruellan, talking about not being able to enjoy his first check. Kruellan obviously told him to just go ahead and give Musik the money. Out of anger, he physically threw the money at her, right outside of the doctor's office, in the hallway. Musik was so embarrassed, and no, she didn't pick it up. Kruellan was truly one of a kind. Whether her son was right or wrong, she had his back.

Later on that day, she called Musik and made it seem as if Musik was in the wrong for asking Ramon to help pay for their daughter's doctor visit. Musik had paid for all the doctor visits up until that moment. That's just how Kruellan was, and eventually, Musik just accepted who she was and knew what kind of things she was capable of doing.

But talking about who could cook, that woman cooked so well that she should have opened up her own restaurant! Kruellan made the meanest buttermilk pies and fed Musik throughout her entire pregnancy, so Musik appreciated her for that. She was nice one minute and then cruel and cursing you out the next. If her son had an issue with you, you immediately became her issue.

Ramon and Musik argued, fussed, and fought for the majority of the time when it was time to pay bills. Ramon wrecked one of Musik's vehicals, drove another one into water, and drove the front of another one into the side of a garage. From Musik being slapped in the face, to being choked until she blacked out, she thought she had reached her breaking point. Musik gave birth to their beautiful princess, Piper, after two hot bowls of gumbo. She thought things would calm down until Ramon was caught openly flirting with that same ex-girlfriend of his on social media one week after Musik had given birth to their daughter. He told his ex that he was thinking of her and missed her. She responded with a smiley face. That, among other things, did it for Musik, so she told him that she was not for him and that he should go ahead and move out.

Piper was only three weeks old at the time. Ramon plotted for some hours on what happened next, and that mother of his, Kruellan, was in on his plan. When nighttime fell, Ramon went to get his belongings out of Musik's apartment. One of his older brothers went along with him to help. Ramon had Kruellan to pretend to be like the Good Samaritan as she contacted Musik multiple times to make sure she was home, and then she told her to just let him in to get his belongings. It was weird because Musik had already agreed on allowing Ramon in to get his belongings. While Ramon was packing his belongings, his brother asked Musik if he could hold Piper. Musik knew that he wouldn't harm Piper, so she allowed him to do so. Ramon then asked Musik if the two of them could go into her bedroom and talk before he left.

A few minutes later, a phone call came through on Ramon's cell phone. He grabbed their daughter's baby bag, which was sitting on Musik's bed, and ran out of the apartment. As Musik approached the living room, Piper and her car seat were gone. She ran to Piper's closet, and all of Piper's baby clothes were gone. She then took off running full speed down the stairs to get her baby, but her uncle had already driven off with her. Musik saw Ramon at the exit gate of the apartments and ran to the car he was in. She began beating on the window and pulling the door handle, trying to stop him.

All she could do was cry and ask him what he was doing. The harder she beat on the window, the weaker her body became. He sped off. Musik jumped into her own vehicle and attempted to chase him down but lost him. She called Grandmother Fay, crying, telling her that they took her baby from her! She then called 911, but they couldn't even help her because there were no court orders in place. However, one of the female officers did give her some very helpful advice. Her advice was for Musik to sweet talk Piper's father into coming back to her apartment.

She told her to do what she had to do in order to get her daughter back into her arms.

Musik blew Ramon's phone up, close to or a little bit over a hundred times, per the female officer's advice, but he did not answer nor reply. It took everything in her not to lose her mind. She also called Kruellan, who knew what was going on the entire time but played along with the game that Ramon was playing. The next day, Musik went on a search for Piper herself. She drove to every possible place that Ramon could possibly be, even to the house of Ramon's brother—the brother who had helped Ramon kidnap Piper. They were there, and she knew it because they called her as soon as they saw her sitting on the car that Piper was kidnapped in.

Ramon tried to lie by telling Musik that they were not there, but she pulled out of the apartment as if she was leaving and just waited. She saw them getting into the vehicle that they kidnapped Piper in and then leaving out of a different gate. Musik couldn't catch them, but she knew for sure that it was them because Ramon had on the same exact work clothes that he had on the night before when they kidnapped Piper.

Up until that point, Kruellan had been answering Musik's phone calls yet still playing along with Ramon's act of foolishness. Musik knew that she was in on their plan when she started forwarding her phone calls to voicemail. Musik confirmed that she was in on the plan through two pictures that she had requested at two different times—one from Ramon and one from Kruellan. Musik was already doing what the female officer suggested for her to do, by sweet-talking Ramon into coming back to her apartment. She told him that she missed Piper and just wanted a picture. He sent her a picture of Piper by a windowsill, laying on a familiar blanket. Later on that night, Kruellan finally called her back, telling her that she now had Piper. The funny thing was that Musik also asked her to send her a picture of Piper because she was really missing her. Kruellan sent her a picture of Piper by the same windowsill, laying on that same familiar blanket. At this point, Musik knew that Piper had been over there with Kruellan since morning time when they had snuck away from the house of Ramon's brother, and just started playing right along with them. The good thing was that she knew that Piper was safe and that Kruellan wouldn't do anything to harm her. That gave her a little peace of mind. More days had passed, and Musik was still working on getting her daughter back home.

Nothing in her soul trusted Ramon, so she went ahead and filed a court order so that he would never be able to take Piper away from her again. Ramon felt more in control by telling Musik that she would never see her daughter again. Two weeks and three days later, Piper was back home. Musik could never see herself forgiving Ramon for what he had done to her. She had been breastfeeding Piper, and when Ramon decided to kidnap her, he put her on formula. Musik had to pray harder and harder to keep her mouth shut and her mind stable. She thanked the Lord that he kept her in her right mind. Musik was grateful that during that entire incident her son England was safe at the home of Grandmother Fay. It was Jesus, and him only, who pulled her through that mess.

Things calmed down for a while, but things were different. Musik was different, and Ramon noticed. She felt as if there was nothing more that anyone could do to her—to hurt her more than what she had already been through. She found herself just there, having a spotless mind. The days without Piper, Musik locked herself in her room, by herself, and tried not to fall deeper into depression. She cried like a baby until she could no longer feel her face. This situation made her grow up a little bit more. She was now even stronger and prepared for anything that was going to happen next.

One night Musik was at Grandmother Fay's house, braiding her younger sister Lyra's hair, and she made sure to communicate with Ramon in terms of her whereabouts. When she arrived home, he started a pointless argument, saying that she had Piper out in the night air too late. Musik even reminded him that she was consistently communicating with him throughout the night, by calling him every hour to make him aware of how much longer she had to work on Lyra's hair. She even called him when she was on her way home.

When she arrived home, she packed England and Piper up the stairs, with Piper in her car seat on her right arm and England on her left hip. She called Ramon to come help her get the babies out of the car, but he did not answer the phone. When she finally made it up the stairs and into the apartment, he went off on her, cursing her out and calling her out of her name. Musik didn't feel like arguing, especially since she had both of her babies with her, so she turned around and proceeded to leave out the front door and to return back to her grandparents' house. He then got up off the couch on which he was laying, walked over to

Musik, pushed the door shut, and said, "Bitch, you can take your son, but not my motherfucking daughter."

She told him that he didn't have to call her out of her name, especially in front of the kids. He called her bitch again, and she then called him one back. He threatened her and told her to call him bitch again. She told him that if he called her one again, she would call him one back. So he called her bitch again, and when she called him one back this time, he pulled back and slapped her so hard in her face. He then told her to call him another one. He called her bitch once again, and she called him one back. This time, he slapped her even harder.

Musik felt so powerless standing there and worthless. All she could say to him as she began to cry was, "really? In front of my babies with the both of them in my arms?" The first slap shocked England, and the second slap made him cry and scream to the top of his lungs. Musik didn't fight back because she knew that night she could have possibly lost both of her babies, if the police had to get involved. So she sat both England and Piper in their room and turned on their television as she sat on the couch and cried. England came out of their room a few minutes later and came to sit by Musik on the couch. Without saying a word, he wiped Musik's tears and then laid his head on her shoulder. England was only two years old at the time.

Another time after that, Ramon and Musik were into it, and every time she tried to stand up from the couch, he pushed her in her chest hard, multiple times, telling her to sit her ass down and then daring her to stand back up. At this point, she wondered if prison had really jacked his head up.

These are all the things that Musik had to deal with while teaching her high school students at Victory High School. Another obstacle she had to overcome was one time when she went home on her lunch break. Another argument was sparked due to England's father wanting to go visit him at Grandmother Fay's house, and it of course, turned into a physical altercation. Musik had to return back to work, stand in front of her students, and teach as if everything was okay. She was so torn apart on the inside. She grew even angrier because he went lying about her to his family and turning them against her in order to justify why he was abusive and allergic to paying bills. She just had to take the good with the bad and found herself peaceful when she stopped worrying about how she was perceived by them and others.

CHAPTER 12

Is Enough Really Enough When You're Finally Fed Up?

AFTER ALL THAT had transpired, Musik still tried to hold on, with hopes of things eventually getting better. They never did. She thought Ramon would change. He never did. They temporarily broke up again, but this time, he took a few more stabs to her heart. Ramon knew that Victory High School only paid Musik once a month. He left at the beginning of the month and cleared out the cabinets, taking all the food. He was consistently starting to hang out at another one of his brother's apartments. Musik figured it was another woman because his behavior toward her changed. She figured right when it was brought to her attention that he could possibly be messing with the leasing agent at his brother's apartments.

Musik and Ramon agreed to take space, but they were not officially broken up and would not take sex out of the equation, agreeing to not engage in any sexual activity with anyone else. But in the meantime, he would be staying at his brother's apartment. The female knew about Musik and Ramon's relationship but was still bold enough to take a picture in some of his sunglasses and put it on social media. Musik couldn't get mad at her because that girl didn't owe her anything. Her name was Tayah.

Musik was on her way to being fed up on the day she went to those apartments in search of the truth. While approaching Tayah, she let her know that she was not there to fight or harm her, but she only wanted the truth. This was one of those days again when Musik asked God to show her the truth no matter how bad it would hurt. He did just that, again. As she sat with Tayah, the first thing Musik noticed was how beautiful she was. Tayah had beautiful, flawless skin; a beautiful smile; and beautiful hair—the kind that naturally curls up when you wet it, and it was hers. She was so gorgeous that she had Musik second-guessing herself. Tayah was so good looking that if Musik was a man, she would have messed with her herself.

Her first question to Tayah was whether or not she and Ramon had been messing around. She needed to know because Musik and Ramon were still sexually active. Musik then asked Tayah to tell her the truth because she knew for a fact that she wouldn't get it from Ramon. Her knees became weak as Tayah finally came clean and nodded yes. She then asked Tayah the last time they had been active, because Ramon and Musik were just active the day before. Tayah admitted to Musik that she and Ramon had been active during that same week. Musik's stomach turned. Tayah then went on, telling Musik that Ramon had been staying with her at her apartment and not at his brother's apartment. She also mentioned to Musik that Ramon had one of his ex-girlfriends in Musik's car while Musik was at work. She told Musik that Ramon also had sex with his ex-girlfriend and chilled with his ex in her apartment. Musik figured that the day Ramon came to pick her up from work extremely late, was the day Tayah was referring to. Just like she knew he had sex with a female in her car the day he came to pick her up from work and had removed both of the kids' car seats from the back seat of her car. On top of that, her car had a very distinct and unpleasant odor! She now understood why her principal at the time, Ms. Gilmore, would always tell her, "Ms. Raine, keep that boy out of your car . . . he ain't right!" Everything started to make sense now and went downhill from there. Musik told Tayah to call Ramon to the office because she wanted to see what he had to say. That's where she messed up. She had all the answers that she was looking for, so she should have just left and completely separated herself from him.

He came in the office, and by this time, Musik had just given birth to their Piper five months prior to this incident, so she still had baby weight on her. He was caught, and at that point in time, he looked at her and told her that he did not want her and then looked at Tayah and told her that he wanted her instead. Musik looked at Tayah and said, "It's just a matter of time before he does to you exactly what he is doing to me, from the abuse on down."

Ramon then told Tayah that he would never hit her because she wasn't Musik. He began to beg Tayah and asked her to still be with him, in front of Musik, and then he got mad the more she ignored him. He showed his true colors when he started coming out of his hoodie, hitting his fist at Musik, telling her that he was about to beat her ass. He snatched Musik's keys from her, and Musik snatched his phone. He threw her keys on the top of a carport across the street.

As soon as Tayah turned and walked the opposite way, he ran toward Musik and punched her, with all his might, in her jaw. He had already called his sister over to attempt to fight Musik. Musik called the police on him, not her. His sister, of course, took up for him, and her choice of words she used toward Musik, in this particular situation, was hurtful because Musik thought that the two of them were better than that. She was different from their mother, Kruellan, because she would always be on the side of right and would stay away from getting in between whatever transpired between Ramon—her brother and Musik.

The next day was a Sunday, and Ramon's sister personally approached Musik to apologize for her actions. She told Musik that she had been through what she had just experienced before. As a woman, Ramon's sister knew that she caused more hurt and that she shouldn't have reacted that way. His mother, on the other hand, of course, blew Musik's phone up, cursing her out and threatening to physically harm her if her son was to go back to prison.

It's funny how God will make a situation so uncomfortable if that situation is not for you. He will allow things to become so uncomfortable to the point where you have no choice but to get out. This is truly a dog-eat-dog world. It turned out that Tayah was the best friend of the ex-girlfriend that Ramon had in Musik's car. Things never got better because he was never for Musik to begin with. Musik should have listened to the prophet that came to church and told her, years before Ramon was released from prison, to let him go because he did not need to benefit from her. The prophet didn't know Musik nor Ramon, but he knew how to listen to the voice of God. Shame on Musik for not listening!

Musik finally had enough, a year later—the night before Mother's Day. She looked in the mirror and told herself that, that particular night was the last night that she would waste her tears on Ramon. She pulled herself together and realized that she had two children to live for and that it was time to let him go, especially when he told her that he didn't have to celebrate Mother's Day with her because she wasn't his mother. Musik was not materialistic at all. She always believed that it was the thought that counts. So, she would have been thankful to at least received a homemade card. On top of that, the abuse continued, so Musik had no choice but to get out.

This was the relationship where everything went black, and she fell to the ground, clutching her stomach, praying to God that her unborn child—their daughter Piper, was okay. In this particular relationship, arguments led to her being slapped to the ground, being choked until she blacked out, and having her head bashed into doors and the floor on which she now lay, multiple times. Blows to her face and chest left her breathless and in pain, scared to fight back out of fear of losing her babies—both England and Piper. That was not the first time.

Neither was it the last. However, she noticed that each and every current situation prepared her for a future-present situation. Things got worse before they got better. She's, however, grateful for Ramon being a good father to Piper. All that they went through no longer matters; however, their daughter's happiness does. So whenever Ramon calls for Piper, she goes, regardless of what the court order says. This relationship taught Musik to put a limit on her tears.

CHAPTER 13

Happily Ever After and Many Happy Hours Needed

AFTER THE STORMS and hurricanes that flooded her life and nearly sucked all the life out of her, Musik finally met the perfect guy. She was still living in California but was now working at Level Up Academy, under the leadership of Dr. Sanders—her principal at the time—a phenomenal woman. The perfect guy's name was Trent, and he was years older than her. But they both found commonality in college band and then through a college band fraternity and sorority. Their first date was remarkable as he opened every single door that she stepped through. He had a two-story house, gave his mother a Mercedes-Benz for her birthday and gave his father a nice truck for Father's Day. None of the materialistic things attracted Musik to him; however, she just couldn't figure out why he deemed it necessary to shine light on all his possessions. She fell in love with his beginning willingness to make her happy and with the good she saw in him. Trent mentioned that he would soon be packing his belongings from his home and moving back home with his mother, in order to save money.

During the summer months, Musik applied for another teaching job at Christa McAuliffe Middle School under Principal Mary Brewster. She had also recently moved in with Grandmother Fay to start saving for a home for herself and her two babies at the time, so they both had an understanding. Musik and Trent were both comfortable with their blended family size as she had mentioned and made it clear to him that she was not ready for another kid at the time. She had also made him aware that she was not on any type of birth control. He promised to be careful during the times they did not use protection.

A few months later, she was late, with a positive pregnancy test. When she questioned him about it, all he could say was that he wanted a family with her, and that was why he got her pregnant. How was Musik unaware? He supposedly orgasmed once, but it was actually twice—the first time inside but played off and the second time pulled out. Musik was upset, even more so hurt, but could not bear the thought of getting an abortion. Her positive pregnancy test showed her a side of this man that she never thought she would see.

She received a phone call from the associate principal, at Christa McAuliffe Middle School and went on an interview. They hired her. Months later, Trent and Musik got engaged and then got married not too much longer after that. They were not ready and should have stay engaged a lot longer. The signs were there, but Musik ignored them, trying to give this man a chance.

As time passed, lying became one of Trent's best traits but also an abuse trigger once confronted. His initial act of physical abuse took place when he forgot one of his lies. Musik calmly brought it to his attention, with concrete proof, which lead to her getting choked against the wall in her grandparents' garage by Trent. Her grandparents were both upstairs, but Piper—two years old at the time, walking in on him performing that act, caused a different level of pain. So now both of Musik's babies—England and Piper, had witnessed their mother being physically abused on two different occasions, from two different men. That moment was the moment Musik should have walked away, but she found herself blaming herself for his abuse toward her and then believing him when he said that he wouldn't do it again. He promised to change, but he never did.

Months down the line, things seemed to get a little better. The two of them decided to take things a little bit further and rented a home that was big enough for his five kids plus her two kids, and soon to be three. Musik was finding happiness again until all the weight, all at once, fell on her shoulders yet again.

Before Trent and Musik moved in together, Musik drafted up a budget that split the main bills in half. Trent took a look at the budget and said that he could afford his portion. It wasn't until after they moved in together and after they were married that she realized that something was wrong. Trent's bi-weekly pay was not matching the hours he was claiming to work, and he paid as less as possible on his portion of the bills, which made Musik have to make up the difference. Trent quit one of his jobs, found another one that paid more money, and still decided to hide money.

After sitting down and speaking with the parents of Trent, the truth came out about everything. It was brought to Musik's attention that Trent did not know how to pay bills because he had never really lived on his own. He would buy shoes and hide them at his parents' house, get extensions on the light bills when he had the money, and then lie to Musik about the amount of money he had, which made him short on his half of the rent. After counseling with his parents, she prayed and hoped that things would get better. As time passed, he started improving on the finances, but the lying, infidelity, and abuse continued.

During her pregnancy, whenever a lie came out, his defense was abuse. Social media was a priority to him. Let's just say, if Trent had to choose between Musik and social media, Musik would go and social media would stay. The two of them got into arguments dealing with multiple women from his social media—whether he was reaching out to them to flirt or to initiate conversation. When he was caught, they were either his cousins or females before Musik. A guy who acts single while he is married was never ready for marriage to begin with and should just remain single. Positive conversations are harmless, until the intent behind the conversations prove to be perverted.

Trent tried to talk Musik into getting an abortion. He knew that she did not believe in abortion; however, that's what he wanted her to do at the time. She could not understand how he admitted to getting her pregnant on purpose because he wanted a family with her and then turned right around and wanted her to get an abortion. She was his wife! What kind of husband admits to getting his wife pregnant on purpose and then tries to make her get an abortion?

Musik couldn't figure out, for the life of her, how she managed to get into the same exact situation twice, in back-to-back relationships. She found herself again having to pay for her now third child's birth alone. Trent wanted to name their child after a woman that he previously had a crush on if the baby was a girl. This was beyond an insult, so when Musik told him no and then offered for them to sit down together to come up with baby names, he declined, and he then used this particular situation as a crutch as to why he didn't help her pay for any of the remaining doctor bills. Thank God, they had a boy!

Musik was overwhelmed, but when her students at Christa McAuliffe Middle School flooded her with thank-you notes, she remembered how very blessed she still was. Notes from them always managed to come right on time. It felt good to feel appreciated. It's like they always knew when Ms. Raine needed some encouraging words. She will forever love them for the love they showed her throughout her pregnancy, not knowing the hell she was going through at home.

Musik did not know what it was about her and her seventh month of pregnancy, but again, now in her marriage, things took a turn for the worse. On the way to a Christmas party, Trent picked an argument about whose car they were going to drive to the Christmas party. Her response to him was that she did not care whose car they drove as long as they put gas in the car. Come to find out, he picked an argument that night so that he could get rid of Musik to go have sex with one of his baby mamas. Musik was hormonal and was crying as he cursed her out, and she mentioned that Trent had to be guilty of something because she did nothing to him for the entire weekend to trigger his current actions. Trent told her, while driving on a tollway, that she could get her motherfucking ass out of his car. Musik then told him that she was worth more than that and that he didn't have to talk to her that way. Trent then told Musik to shut her crybaby ass up and drove all the way back to their home, with hopes that he could get her to willingly get out of his car so that he could meet up with that particular baby mama. Trent's baby mama's name was Deviline. During this time, Musik was big and pregnant. It took her a good minute—okay . . . maybe about an hour—to get dressed, so she was going to somebody's party.

This was by far the worst pregnancy experience that Musik had encountered. She was married but had to do the entire pregnancy without her husband's support. He consistently made time for what was important to him, and it was obviously never Musik. She was only good enough for his leftover time. Many nights, she silently cried in the shower and asked God what she had gotten herself into. Musik could hear God's voice telling her that she should have trusted him enough to wait on him, instead of making her own decisions with his consent. She then prayed for God to get her out! Other nights, she would just sing to make herself happy and then rock herself to sleep as she cuddled with her two pregnancy pillows.

Musik was so stressed out and was suffering from kidney stones. Their son Harley was born premature, at five pounds and a few ounces. Right before she went into the labor-and-delivery room, a doctor came in to do one last ultrasound. Earlier that day, Harley was head down, and Musik mentioned that to the doctor. However, the doctor told Musik that something was telling him to still do one last ultrasound. To their surprise, within the matter of a few hours, Harley had turned breech. He wanted to come out feet first. Musik delivered her other two babies, England and Piper, vaginally, but Harley decided to flip and caused Musik to have to have a Cesarean section. When he came out, he had the umbilical cord wrapped around his neck twice. Yes, he was indeed her miracle baby and meant to be here.

Some nights, Musik would call and talk to England's other mom, Monisha, to vent. She was another phenomenal woman. She is actually England's stepmother, and Musik respects her for treating England as her own son. When Musik was in the hospital giving birth to Harley, Monisha took time out of her busy schedule on Easter weekend to pick up England and took him to get a haircut for Easter Sunday. Of course, Musik and Monisha had a few disagreements over the years, but eventually, they worked through them all. Peace is a gift!

Musik didn't find out about Trent cheating on her until four months after she had given birth to Harley. He ended up cheated on Musik with Deviline anyways and was determined to hide it. One morning, while Musik was teaching summer school, she and Deviline had a conversation over the phone. Deviline admitted to Musik that Trent had been trying to have sex with her. He was married to Musik but sending Deviline nude pictures of himself and then begging her for nude pictures in return. She sent him a nude picture and lied about it, but she didn't owe Musik anything. Musik's commitment was to Trent, not Deviline. Other screenshots exposed that he was asking her if he could come slide his penis in her and also offering to massage her feet and rub her back—things that Musik could never get from him.

Trent had a really hard time being honest, and when he noticed himself that his lies weren't making sense, he would attempt to blame Musik for why he was lying to her. Trent abused Musik on her first day back to work from maternity leave, and sent her a cocky text message, reading, "Sorry I brought this upon you on your first day back to work. I can accept full responsibility and call the police or leave so that this will never happen again. Here's the proof you need, that I abused you." Musik was at work, on lunch break, when she read that text message from Trent. Musik's neck was bruised, and her lips were busted.

Another time, Trent punched Musik in her chest, and popped her arm out of place, bruising it, which caused her to have to wear long-sleeved shirts again to cover up her bruises. He got caught in a lie once about the purchasing of a $750 cell phone, that caused him to not have his portion of the rent again, and became abusive when confronted. Musik asked him why he felt the need to lie. He then attempted to turn the tables, by threatening her, saying, "Call me a liar again and see if I don't wipe that motherfucking smirk from your face."

Trent turned into a monster whenever he got caught in a lie. His reaction every single time, in order to control the situation, was to physically attack. He also attempted to break Musik down mentally. She was told by him that she was mentally unattractive to him; that he was not attracted to her pregnant body, especially one to two months after giving birth to Harley; and that she had a pregnant-looking stomach. The put-downs became worse. He even admitted to her that he followed a naked woman on his social media just to look at her slim, sexy body. The girl did have a nice, slim, and sexy body, but Trent took disrespect to another level.

It was Musik's birthday weekend when she realized that she just may have not been his type. Two days after her birthday, they fought and tussled all the way until it was time for her to leave and report to work. It just happened to be Award's Day at Christa McAuliffe Middle School. She was so spaced out and could barely see because he had slapped her contacts out of her eyes. She had to put on an old pair of her glasses that were definitely not her correct prescription.

Another incident occurred while they were in the middle of a physical altercation. The night ended with Trent roughly grabbing Musik and throwing her onto her bed face down, pulling her pants down. The more she lifted up, the harder he pushed her down to the bed. She was crying, and she told him that he was hurting her as he pushed himself inside of her. He didn't stop. When he orgasmed, he pulled himself out and went into their living room. He made her bleed! Musik followed him into the living room, asking him what had just transpired. He responded by saying that he didn't know. Musik asked him what he meant by "he didn't know." He then responded by saying that he didn't know and that it just happened. She told him that he was so wrong for doing that to her. She returned to her bed and just laid there. She couldn't sleep that night, and she still had to report to work the next morning.

That baby momma of his, Deviline, was determined to ruin their marriage. Trent fell right into her trap. Because he knew that he had cheated on Musik with Deviline, he played by her rules, putting Musik on the backburner. He attempted to blame Musik for Deviline going to the attorney general for a review to increase child support. This was the same conversation that led to him attempting to put his hands on Musik again. His daughter, Musik's stepdaughter at the time, came into the room. He grabbed her hand and told her to go into their bedroom closet. As Trent came toward Musik, lifting his hand to hit her, Musik screamed her stepdaughter's name so loud that her stepdaughter came out of the closet. Musik knew Trent didn't want his daughter to see that side of him.

That wasn't Trent's first time abusing Musik while the kids were there. One Sunday, before she left to go do the morning announcements at her church, Trent kept closing doors to block the kids from seeing him choke her, bashing her head into doors, and even pulling her hair. She rushed to church to do the announcements. Musik had to stand in front of the entire church as if nothing was wrong, but on the inside, she was a disaster and hurt to the core. She realized that her husband was married to her but putting his other baby mama first. She's sure that her little stepbabies had an earful to go back and tell their mother, but it is what it is.

Trent would always tell Musik that if she and he didn't make it and ended up getting a divorce, she would be stuck out. Musik should have known that they were not meant to be after bringing in the New Year alone as a first-year married woman.

Musik made a huge mistake by telling Trent about her past relationships and hurts. He knew her past hurt her and managed to repeat exactly what had previously caused her hurt. When Harley arrived, it wasn't until Musik filed child support on Trent that Trent's mother made him purchase a pack of diapers for Harley, for first time. When Musik filed for a divorce, he didn't agree with it and promised to change, but she could no longer trust his words. She had to base her decision off the actions Trent had shown her thus far.

CHAPTER 14

First-Time Wife

AS A FIRST-TIME wife, Musik realized that she didn't provide her husband, Trent, with his peaceful place. She had no book to tell her how to be the perfect wife. She thought that if she cooked, cleaned, made his lunch, and slid nice notes in his lunch from time to time just to tell him that she loved and still appreciated him through it all, that things would get better. She had sex with him whenever he wanted, and that still wasn't enough. Musik didn't understand how he could give advice to a few of her sorority sisters, telling them how not to accept everything that he was doing to her behind closed doors.

Trent was one way in public and another way behind closed doors. He was sweet, charming, and as one of Musik grandmothers would say, "could talk sugar out of coffee." One of his favorite slogans was *Fake the Funk*. Musik now understood why. She eventually stopped him from opening her doors, being that he only consistently opened her doors most of the time when they were in front of people.

It hurt Musik to see how supportive he was to some of his other friends and couples who were expecting a baby, while he left her hanging but made everything look good for and on social media. However, she left out the most important ingredient—God. So much was going on that Musik only prayed when it was convenient for her. God is peace. Musik nagged Trent so much about his mismanagement of money and other women that she failed to make their home his paradise. She never eased up. She wanted answers right then and there. She wanted to know why he cheated and why he lied. This caused her to have an attitude. She should have followed Bruno Mars's advice—threw some perm on her attitude and relaxed. Whatever he was wanting to do, was planning to do, and was currently doing were completely out of her control.

This was Musik's first time being a wife, and she knew that she wasn't perfect. But she always found herself asking him what she could do better. First things first, she had to learn not to bring issues to him while he was on his way to work or while he was at work. She should have understood where he was coming from because he was right, no one appreciates going to work frustrated. Musik felt like if something transpired while he was at work or if he found time to commit an act while he was at work, the issue should have been addressed right then and there. It was the same if ever there was an issue on her end. For example, when one of his frat brothers was flirting with her on one of her social-media pages, Trent called her while she was at work, and she addressed and resolve the issue right then and there, on Trent's timing, not on her own timing.

Trent was her priority, but she was never his, and over time, she had to accept it until she got over it or was ready to move on. Trent told her to block the guy that was flirting with her, and she did just that, immediately. So it was okay for him to call her at work with issues, but it was not okay for her to call him while he was at work with issues. He would always promise to discuss the issues once they arrived home for the evening so that they could move forward. However, that never happened. This led to even more arguments. When the evening came, he would go to sleep and pretend as if he was too tired to talk about the issues at hand. Another one of his ways out was for him to tell Musik that she didn't asked him questions the right way. She could have asked him very calmly why he cheated, and he would say, "You came at me the wrong way," or he would ignore her as if she wasn't there. So none of their issues would get resolved.

Musik was very analytical, so when something was bothering her, she felt as if it was very important to talk about it and to also figure out how and why. However, she realized after this marriage that it wasn't worth it. People are who they are, and if they have their mind set on doing something, they are going to do it, whether you approve of it or not. Musik did not choose her battles wisely.

From Musik finding out that Trent pretended to be at work some days, inviting other women out, offering to buy them drinks, and taking people out to breakfast while he was still short on his portion of their household bills, Musik had no choice but to downsize from their house to an apartment.

From her finding receipts of him stopping to get himself something to eat and then leaving the kids and her to fend for themselves, things were at a point of no return. When Musik purchased food for her babies and herself, she also purchased food for Trent because he was her husband, and it was what she felt was the right thing to do.

Musik soon realized that she should have shut her mouth, kept her emotions under control, and allowed things to just run their course. One of her line sisters, Sharhonda, put it plain and simple when she asked Musik about her next steps after information was brought to her and sat on her lap. She said, "What are you going to do about it? If you are not going to leave the man, leave the situation alone and move on."

Sharhonda was right. No matter how angry Musik became about Trent's lying, cheating, and abuse, if she knew that she was still going to stay with him regardless, any discussion about the issue at hand became irrelevant and was a waste of breath and good energy. This was simply because Trent had already showed Musik his true colors and what he was capable of doing. Just because she was aware of his wrongdoings did not necessarily mean that she was supposed to bring it to his attention. Some things were brought to Musik, only to make her aware and in order for her to guard her heart. Trent too was only human. So like all others, Musik had to forgive Trent, not for him but for herself.

CHAPTER 15

Resilience

NOW AS A single mother of three, with all three of her babies baring different last names, being strong is Musik's only option. As she pulls into her garage, she gets out of her vehicle and stares at three pairs of eyes looking back at her. She now has to unload England, Piper, and baby Harley and get them upstairs into her apartment. As she looks at them, she is reminded so much of their fathers, in which is now a beautiful thing. Sometimes, we, as humans, are so focused on the bad that we fail to recognize the beauty in the struggle that we once appreciated before things turned sour.

England is smart, loving, goofy, bossy, and has his father's walk and personality. At the same time, he is a perfectionist. Sometimes he thinks that he is the father of his two younger siblings and wants them to do exactly as he says. However, Musik's one and only daughter, Piper, has her own brain and does the exact opposite of whatever England tells her to do. Either way it goes, Harley, her baby boy, is thinking of a master plan to figure out how to get things to go his way.

Piper is a spitting image of her father, two of her best features being her smile and that crazy-sounding laugh that Musik will now never be able to escape. Piper provides Musik with the juiciest kisses, while England provides her with the warmest hugs. Harley has his father's eyes and face and only Musik's skin complexion. Musik believes that Harley is the most dramatic, and she loves every bit of it.

On rough nights, Musik tries her best not to get frustrated as she travels up and down the stairs, unloading groceries. She takes England, Piper and Harley up first. Musik then makes multiple trips from her car upstairs to her apartment and then back down for the next round of groceries, packing as many bags as she can fit on both of her arms at once.

When all the groceries have been put away, she feeds the kids, bathes them, helps them complete all their homework, and then gets them ready for bed. England and Piper have to argue about something before they finally fall asleep, while baby Harley looks at both of them like they are crazy. At the end of every day, Musik is grateful because her babies are her strength. Looking at them every day reminds her of how strong she has to continue to be.

Musik used to feel some type of way as people looked down on her for having three babies by three different men until she realized that what they thought about her was none of her business. She chose life, through all circumstances, over abortions. She made decisions but—as a mother and a woman, period—will continue to work hard every single day. Musik may not be able to give her babies the best of everything or the world, but they will forever get her best, at all times. No matter how many times life knocked her down, Musik recovered quickly. Perseverance was the key. Musik is resilient!

CHAPTER 16

Lessons Learned: "Sweet Sixteen"

PHYSICAL, MENTAL, AND verbal abuse left Musik feeling worthless. Her self-esteem was slowly hitting rock bottom with every blow to her body. No matter how many people told her to get out of certain situations, Musik didn't come out of the situations until she herself was fed up and couldn't bear any more. She noticed that when she came out of situations based on others' opinions and suggestions, she ended up right back in the same situation. Musik found herself saying that she was done with so many situations, so many times. The truth is, Musik was never done until she really had enough. Of course, she felt dumb for staying in hopes that things would work out, but looking back, she has peace knowing that she did everything she could to save the relationships that she committed herself to. As life happened, she learned a lesson every step of the way.

Because life happened, she reflects more and lives by the following "sweet sixteen" principles:

1. "If it ain't peace, it ain't God!" (Bishop Leroy J. Woodard).
2. "No thing and no one are worth your peace of mind" (Jessika C. Hearne).
3. "Don't personalize people's actions. If somebody is not there for you, it's because God doesn't want them to be there for you. If somebody is not in your life, it's because God doesn't want them in your life, and therefore, you're either going to get somebody that you're supposed to have, or something within you is going to be strengthened in their absence" (Valencia D. Clay).
4. "Every saint got a past, every sinner got a future" (J. Cole).
5. "What others think about you, is none of your business" (Anonymous).
6. "No-one can make you feel inferior, without your consent" (Eleanor Roosevelt).
7. "If you lose it, it was either there for you temporarily or never for you at all" (Jessika C. Hearne).
8. "Throw some perm on your attitude, you gotta relax" (Bruno Mars).
9. "No one can take what is meant to belong to you" (Jessika C. Hearne).
10. "Everything that hurt you served its purpose" (Jessika C. Hearne).

11. "You pushing through it all is proof that you are walking resilience" (Jessika C. Hearne).
12. "If a decision brings you peace, you made the right one" (Jessika C. Hearne).
13. "Always give your tears a limit, forgive them, yourself, and then guard your heart" (Jessika C. Hearne).
14. "If they have nothing to lose, lose them" (Jessika C. Hearne).
15. "Connect with people who are not afraid to put you in your place when you are wrong" (Jessika C. Hearne).
16. "A man is only going to change for one woman, and one woman only. If he does not change for you, you are not the one" (Steve Harvey).

CHAPTER 17

So What! Now What?

NO ONE, AND I do mean no one, is responsible for your happiness but you. If ever you depend on others to make you happy, you will forever be one sad individual. Not because you cannot trust everyone but because everyone is human. You too are human, so we all have flaws. We all mess up, and we all hurt and get hurt. But the moment we realize how to recover without hurting others is the moment where we have finally grown up. Everything that Musik encountered in life, everything that she went through, everything that she struggled to overcome, was supposed to happen to her because she is still here. Everything that took place in her life was meant to bend her but never to break her so that she could help others through similar situations. So what, now what?

Musik Raine's goal every single day is to help as many people as she comes into contact with. She is overly blessed to be in the education career field as this is the best opportunity to impact so many individuals every single day. When she experienced her miscarriage, she asked God why he allowed her to lose her baby. A few years later, while teaching ninth- to twelfth-grade math at Victory High School, one of her students was pregnant, and she came to Musik crying, telling her that she had a miscarriage. Musik was able to relate, and she told her student in the most positive way that it just wasn't meant to be.

God answered Musik's question when he sent this student to her. God allowed Musik to experience her miscarriage because he not only knew that she was strong enough to bear that level of hurt but he also knew that somewhere down the line, she would run into a little teenage girl who needed her, and who just happened to be one of her students. Musik was able to ease her student's mind and pain by letting her know that she—Musik, had already experienced what she—the student was now going through. She took advantage of this opportunity to help her student understand all the responsibilities that come along with having a baby, like expensive day care cost, clothes, shoes, diapers, wipes, giving up weekends, no more partying unless a babysitter becomes available, and so forth. Musik then informed her student that this situation could have been a blessing in disguise and that she could be escaping a lot of hurt. Musik's student asked her what she meant by that. Musik then told her that she—her student and her current boyfriend were very young, and there was no way that he could be taking her seriously at such a young age. Musik had her student to think about her possible future, when she's at home tied down with a baby while her boyfriend goes to college, marries, and starts a family with a college-educated woman. The student then expressed to her that she had not looked at her situation in that way.

A few weeks later, the same student ran up to Musik—in which she, of course, called her Ms. Raine—hugged her, thanked her, and told her that she was right. The student was happy that her situation ended how it did once she found out that her now ex-boyfriend was cheating on her and had gotten another young girl pregnant at a different school. This made Ms. Musik Raine smile because what the devil meant for bad, God worked it out for her student's good.

As far as Musik's parents are concerned, she figured they did the best they could with what they had. They are both now excellent grandparents to Musik's three babies and their other grandchildren. Grandmother Fay and Papa Larry are Musik's support system, and she is extremely grateful for them. She works hard every day, trying to become a better version of herself, for herself, and an even better mother for England, Piper, and Harley. Musik Raine is striving hard to make her good, better and her better, best.

Musik Raine met someone new, and he's quite different. He is nothing like what she's used to, and something that she never had before. He is peaceful and amazing at the same time, always reminding Musik to trust the process, and never to rush the process. What does the future hold? Only the universe knows. . .

CHAPTER 18

Chalkboard Talk from Musik Raine's Perspective

Philosophy of Teaching

HAVING THE ABILITY to make a difference makes all the difference. Being an educator is the most honorable and rewarding career in the world, being that we are blessed with the opportunity to change lives every single day, forever! Teaching is my number 1 passion. I love all my students, and they know it because I am sure to tell them that I love them every single day! The days that I may forget, they, of course, are sure to remind me! Children never forget, besides a few homework assignments from time to time, in which I refer to as "help yourself" versus "homework." The feeling you get when all your students who doubted themselves at the beginning of the school year now stand with confidence at graduation as they walk across the stage, closing one and yet beginning the next chapter of their lives, is an irreplaceable feeling.

Reward and praise progress, and that will soon lead to success! Failure will never be an option in the classroom. I have the NY system in full effect. This particular system doesn't believe in the placement of any Fs on any assignment. So instead, the students not meeting standards receive an NY grade, which stands for "Not yet ready to be turned in." When their work meets standards, it is ready to be regraded and entered into the grade book. Through effective use and implementation of a variety of differentiated, instructional strategies, I am always assuring that my lessons and delivery are formatted to reach all learners in a way that is suitable to their individual learning styles. It is of very high importance to always do what is in the best interest of all students. I am forever committed to doing whatever it takes to assure that all my students become successful and lifelong learners.

Educational Issues and Trends

One major issue in public education today is oversize classes that are prone to more distractions and disruptions in terms of discipline. Oversize classes are caused by high turnover rates, which then lead to students being stuck without a permanent core teacher for some or a majority of the academic school year.

Overwhelmed teachers whose passion is replaced with frustration due to the oversize classes and the negative effects that come along with them are another issue. The above issues can be resolved by implementing an effective program in which the focus would be on retaining high quality staff on top of implementing more incentives and appreciation in order to make teachers feel appreciated and valued on a consistent basis. A simple thank you can turn someone's day completely around—from worse to good, better, best!

Lack of parent awareness on the importance and impact of parent involvement on their child's entire educational journey, from grades K to 12, is another issue. For some reason, it is a trend for parents to "bag off" to a certain extent, mainly when their child begins secondary and postsecondary school. In an effort to allow their child to become more independent, they tend to minimize their overall involvement. This issue can be resolved through ongoing communication with the parents and by hosting more educational but fun and informational events that will require parent involvement. Involve parents and make them feel valued, and their involvement will increase and contribute to overall student success.

Lastly, lack of collaboration with the community is an issue. Collaboration with the community is of high importance. Christa McAuliffe's theme this year was TEAM Work. Collaboration is a fancy word for teamwork. TEAM stands for "together everyone achieves more." It truly does take a village to develop a lifelong learner. Collaboration makes carrying the load a little easier.

Teaching Profession

Passion activates the highest level of success as a product. In terms of what I can do to strengthen and improve the teaching profession, I would definitely find a way to reactivate lost passion within great teachers and maximize on the for-sure implementation of differentiated instruction by highly effective teachers. This will be possible through power coaching and professional development on "regaining and maintaining your passion to teach!" This will allow teachers to reflect on reasons they joined the teaching profession. Highly effective teachers are motivated and passionate, and they use different avenues to make learning fun. More of all of the above, would continuously improve the teaching profession.

No one cares about how much you know until they know how much you care. With that being said, a highly effective teacher knows and understands the importance of capturing the hearts of all kids, even the students that they do not currently teach. Students are more likely to learn from who they love and who they know love them back. My students work and perform for me because I set time aside to build positive relationships with them and also their parents.

The building of positive relationships and continuous communication with parents are what create a positive classroom culture, which allows my students to be the very best version of themselves at all times. This also makes teaching them and them being receptive of my teaching a hundred times easier. I would maximize on the for-sure implementation of differentiated instruction because it works, and it is necessary in order to meet all students where they are and then get them to where they should be. Highly effective teachers will always do whatever it takes to ensure that all students are most successful and become lifelong learners. Motivated teachers motivate students!

CHAPTER 19

God's Favor on Musik Raine

ALL AT ONCE, the building principal, Mary Brewster, and the other administrators—Tracy Rich, James Kirkpatrick, and Mrs. Candace Richmond—walked into Musik's classroom and stood as if something terrible had happened. To her surprise, they interrupted her class lecture to announce to her class that she was the Campus Teacher of the Year. Tears flowed down her face because what no one knew at the time was that her home life was a wreck, and she literally felt like the worst teacher of the year. So this was an honor. At the same time, she never allowed her home life to affect her teaching nor her delivery to her students.

Musik then became a District Teacher of the Year finalist, and months later was named the Secondary District Teacher of the Year, for her school district. It's funny how you have all these plans for your life, and then God intervenes with his plan that he has always had for your life before you were even thought of! Now Musik truly understands the difference between a job and a career! She always dreamed of being an attorney until she got burned out and dreaded going to work every day at a trustee's office. It was the same routine every day. For some people, it works out just fine, but she knew that wasn't God's plan for her life! Being an educator gives her so much joy! It's so rewarding to actually be able to impact so many lives other than your own life every single day!

That feeling you get inside the classroom when all your students finally get it! One of Musik's students grew up to be a nurse and ended up giving her three babies their immunizations at the doctor's office. Another one of her students served her food and gave her a *free* large drink from the drive-through window at Wendy's when he looked up and recognized her. To her surprise, he was the manager. Just knowing that they turned out OK and did well for themselves is an irreplaceable feeling! God knows best.

CHAPTER 20

Help More, Hurt Less

AS A MEMBER of Tau Beta Sigma National Honorary Band Sorority and Alpha Kappa Alpha Sorority Incorporated, service-oriented involvement is of high importance. Food drives, toy drives, the hosting of domestic violence events, and a variety of other events that the community would greatly benefit from are just a few to name amongst many other community service events. Musik volunteers as a tutor during enrichment and/or after-school programs. She also volunteers with her church—City Cathedral, during the Thanksgiving Day and Christmas Eve super feasts. At the super feast, along with other volunteers, they help feed and clothe thousands and thousands of homeless persons and families.

Musik admires her campus for the back-to-school community walk in which, this past year, they collaborated with Willowridge High School as they walked the neighborhood in which their students reside, greeting them and their parents and welcoming in the new school year.

Being that Musik and her siblings grew up in poverty, she sees a huge connection between community service and the classroom. It is of high importance to always remember where you came from in order to remain humble. Imagine how students will feel in the classroom if they consistently see you in their community serving outside of the classroom. This would definitely help create a bond like no other and, furthermore, help the students understand that we are all in this together and that we care.

Musik is also proud to say that, for the first time in many years, the Christa McAuliffe cheerleaders, dancers, and baton twirlers were able to march through the community with Willowridge High School for their homecoming parade. As the person responsible for restarting all three teams, along with the other coach, Mica Williams, it was heartwarming to be able to give the community a taste of the CMMS Hawk Spirit! She appreciates Mica Williams for her loyalty and commitment to the team, especially during her maternity leave.

Educators are counselors, motivators, role models, and so forth. In Musik's case, she is sometimes a seamstress on the spot when a student splits his pants, a mesh backpack falls apart, or someone simply comes to school with holes in uniform shirts. To all educators, Musik encourages you and challenges you to speak powerful words and success into all your students' lives and, yes, even the ones who need a little *extra* love! Educators impact so many lives throughout the years, and the words we speak into their lives carry so much weight!

Understand that it is okay to tell your students that you love them because sometimes they only hear those words from you! We never know what they face at home! Help them understand that their current situation is not their final destination. Inspire. Equip. Imagine. Make supreme success their reality!

At times, it is a struggle to leave work at work as an educator. Balancing home life and work life is an ongoing process. Musik's desire and passion is to truly inspire and equip as many students as possible and show them through her life that not even the sky is the limit. Her most significant contributions in education are her heart and passion to help all students, and people in general, that she may come into contact with.

Her story symbolizes the fact that teachers, just like students, also deal with things at home that are beyond anyone's imagination. Ask her. She can relate to it all because she was them. Life behind the chalkboard.

INDEX

A

Abby (author's relative), viii
abuse, 62–63, 68–69, 79
AD (author's relative), viii
AJ (author's relative), viii
Alexus (Musik's line sister), 45
Alicia (Musik's line sister), 45
Alpha Kappa Alpha Sorority Incorporated, 105
Alvin (author's uncle), viii
american girls Club, 13
Angel (author's aunt), viii
Angie (Musik's line sister), 45
Ann (Musik's grandmother), 8, 29, 36
Antoiniece (Musik's line sister), 45
Ariana (Musik's line sister), 45
Arnecia (Musik's line sister), 45
Ashley (author's relative), viii
Ashley (Musik's line sister), 45
atlanta, 12, 28, 33, 36, 39, 50, 53
Austin (author's relative), viii

B

B, Mr., ix
Bacon (author's friend), ix
Baker (author's friend), ix
Balque (Musik's teacher), 24
band, 23–24, 27, 33, 41, 45
Barack Obama University (BOU), 33–34, 36, 50
Barbara (author's grandmother), viii
Blair (baton twirling coach), 24
Bobbie Jean (author's great-grandmother), viii
Bobby's World, 12
Booker-Brown, Tanea, ix
Boyd (Musik's teacher), 24
Bradford (chief), 24
Braxton (Musik's teacher), 24
Brewster, Mary, ix, 67, 101
Broderick (author's relative), viii
Brumfield family, viii
Bruno Mars (singer), 77
Budd (math teacher), ix

C

Cain (Musik's teacher), 24
California, 3, 36, 53, 67
Campbell (Musik's teacher), 24
Camryn (author's relative), viii
Carey (author's uncle), viii
Carmen Vanguard High School, 27
Champ-JR (author's relative), viii
Charlize (Musik's co-worker), 40–41, 50
Chester (author's uncle), viii
Chicago, 13
Chicago Town State University, 39
Chris (author's relative), viii
Christa Mcauliffe Middle School, 67, 69, 96
Christian (author's relative), viii
Chunte (author's aunt), viii
City Cathedral Church, vii–viii

Clark (author's grandfather), viii
Clay, Valencia D., 87
Coach Baker, 24
Coats, Joselyn, ix
Cole, J., 87
Conner, Larry (author's relative), viii
Conner, Sharon (author's relative), viii
Conner, Tracy (author's relative), viii
Connie (author's relative), viii
Cooper Family, viii
Criminal Justice High School, 27

D

Danielle (author's relative), viii
Daniels (math teacher), ix
Danny (author's nephew), viii
Danny (author's uncle), viii
Daphne (Musik's line sister), 45
Darian (author's relative), viii
Darla (Jameson's mother), 7–8
Dave (Rose's boyfriend), 13, 17–19, 34
Davis (Musik's sixth-grade English teacher), 24, 45
Davis (Musik's teacher), 24
Debboun, Natalie, ix
Dedrick (Musik's best friend), 33
DeFlora-Johnson (author's friend), ix
DeGeneres, Ellen, x
Deshara (Musik's line sister), 45
Destined for Greatness Elementary, 12
Devante (author's relative), viii
Deviline (Trent's mistress), 70–72
Dillard, Ty, viii
Dior (Musik's line sister), 45
divorce, 12, 19, 34, 73
Domonique (author's relative), viii
Duanna Ann (author's relative), viii

Dupre, Charles (superintendent), ix
Dupre, Mrs. (superintendent's wife), ix

E

Emerald (Musik's line sister), 45
England (Musik's first son), 49–50, 53, 57–58, 68, 70–71, 83, 92
Esther (author's aunt), viii
Evelyn (Musik's line sister), 45

F

Falco (Musik's teacher), 24
Fay (Musik's grandmother), 8, 12–13, 27, 50, 55, 57–58, 67, 92
Fed (author's grandmother), viii
Fort Bend Independent School District, x
Franklin (Musik's professor), 24

G

Gangloff (karate instructor), 23
Geraldine (author's aunt), viii
Gilmore (principal), 62
Gipson (Musik's professor), 24
Gladys (author's aunt), viii
Grear (baton twirling coach), 24
Greg (author's grandfather), viii

H

Harley (Musik's second son), 70–73, 83, 92
Harper (author's second daughter), vii
Harvey, Steve, x, 88
Hatter (author's grandfather), viii

Hatter (author's grandmother), viii
Hatter Family, viii
Hearne, Jodeci, viii
Hearne, Joseph, III, viii
Hearne, Joseph, IV, viii
Hearne, Joseph "Jojo," viii
Hearne, Raivyn, viii
Hearne, Zamar, viii
Hearne Family, viii
Herman (Musik's teacher), 24
Hooks, Alesha, viii
Hope Middle School, 23
Howard, Billy "JR," viii
Hunter (band secretary), 45
Hurd Family, viii

I

Ioda (Musik's teacher), 24

J

Jackie (author's aunt), viii
Jackson, Constance, 24
Jacob (author's relative), viii
Jameson (Darla's son), 7
Jasmine (Musik's line sister), 45
Jawntreice (author's relative), viii
Jerry (author's uncle), viii
Jesse Hills High School, 39–40
Jocelyn (author's aunt), viii
Johnson (Musik's professor), 24
Johnson, Teresa, ix
Joseph (Musik's teacher), viii, 24, 33

K

Kaydon (author's nephew), viii

Kayla (Musik's line sister), 45
Keara (Musik's line sister), 45
Keener (baton twirling coach at BOU), 24
Kendal (Musik's friend), 33
Kendra (author's relative), viii
Kerri (author's relative), viii
Kierra (author's relative), viii
Kimberly (author's aunt), viii
Kirkpatrick, James, ix, 101
Kruellan (Ramon's mother), 54–56, 62

L

Laila (Musik's cousin), 35
Latricia (Musik's line sister), 45
Lee (band director), 45
Lee (Musik's professor), 24
Letcher (Musik's teacher), 13, 24
Level Up Academy, 67
Lewis family, viii
Love Independent School District, 12

M

Malone, Courtnie, viii
Malone, Robbin, viii
Malone Family, viii
Mandy (Musik's line sister), 45
Mark (author's relative), viii
Martin, Cheryl, ix
Mary (author's relative), viii
miscarriage, 91
Mississippi, 49
Mitchell (author's relative), viii
Monica (author's relative), viii
Monisha (England's stepmother), 71
Myers (Musik's teacher), 24

N

Natalie (author's aunt), viii
Nick (author's uncle), viii

O

Olford, Tiffany, ix
Oliver Family, viii

P

Paige (Musik's aunt), 19, 35
Paryss (author's first daughter), vii
passion, 23, 95–96, 106
Patricia (Musik's line sister), 45
Penson (band director), 23–24
Perry, Tyler, x
Phylisia (author's relative), viii
Piper (Musik's daughter), 55–57, 62, 64, 68, 70, 83, 92
pregnancy, 49, 54, 69–70
President Classic, 39

R

Raine, Demi, 3, 8, 11, 29, 35
Raine, Harmony, 3, 8, 11, 23, 27, 29–30, 34–36
Raine, Harp, 3–4, 7–8, 11–12, 17, 19, 27–29, 33–34, 49
Raine, Lyra, 3, 8, 11, 29, 35
Raine, Musik
  babies of, 68, 83
  birthday of, 19
  family of, 3
  marriage of, 67
Raine, Quintus, 3, 11, 17, 29
Raine, Rose, 3–4, 7–8, 11–13, 17–19, 29, 33–34
Ramon (Musik's boyfriend), 28–29, 53–58, 61–64
Raphy (Musik's line sister), 45
Reed (Musik's boyfriend), 49–50
Regina (author's aunt), viii
Renata (author's aunt), viii
Rich, Tracy, ix, 101
Richmond, Candace, ix, 101
Roberts, Dave (author's grandfather), viii
Roosevelt, Eleanor, 87

S

Sarafin (Musik's teacher), 23–24
Sasha (Musik's aunt), 19, 35–36
Schell (author's relative), viii
Serena (Musik's line sister), 45
Sharhonda (Musik's line sister), 45, 78–79
Shelton (Musik's teacher), 24
Shy (Musik's prophyte), 45
Singleton (Musik's professor), 24
sisterhood, 43, 45
Smith, Cristine, ix
Smith (Musik's first-grade teacher), 13, 24
Solomon (music teacher), 12
Solomon-Keys-Terry (Musik's teacher), 24
Sonia (author's relative), viii
sorority, 45, 67
Sosa, Juan, ix
Stoner, Derrick, ix
Stoner, La'Jatienne, ix
Strawder (math teacher), ix

Study Hills Independent School District, 23
success, 95–96, 106

T

Tammy (author's relative), viii
Tasha (author's relative), viii
Tau Beta Sigma National Honorary Band Sorority, 45, 105
Tayah (Ramon's fling), 61–63
Taylor, Erma (author's grandmother), viii
Terrance (author's uncle), viii
Terrance Jr. (author's relative), viii
Thomas (author's uncle), viii
Thompson, Stephanie, viii
Thrash, Taura, viii
Tierra (author's relative), viii
Tiffany (author's relative), viii
Tim (author's relative), viii
Toodie (author's relative), viii
Tracy (author's uncle), viii, 101
Tramell II (author's son), vii
Trent (Musik's husband), 67–73, 77–79
Trevin (author's relative), viii
Treyvon (author's relative), viii
truth, 11, 27–28, 61, 68
Trustee David And Sandra Peake, ix
Turner (math teacher), ix
Tyrese (Musik's boyfriend), 39–41
Tyson (author's relative), viii

V

Valerie (author's aunt), viii
Verronica (author's grandmother), viii
Victory High School, 53, 58, 61, 91

W

Walter (author's uncle), viii
Ward (Musik's teacher), 24
Warren (author's uncle), viii
Waymon (author's grandfather), viii
Webber (baton twirling coach), 24
Wilburn Family, viii
Will (author's aunt), viii
William (Musik's grandfather), 8, 29, 36
Williams, Mica, ix, 105
Willowridge High School, 105
Wilson, Barbara (MD), x
Winfrey, Oprah, x
Woodard, Future, viii
Woodard, Leroy J., vii, 87
Woodard Family, viii